I0748141

Every Witch Way but Cursed

Magical Misfits Mysteries - book 17

K.E. O'Connor

K.E. O'Connor Books

ISBN: 978-1-915378-89-7

EVERY WITCH WAY BUT CURSED

Cover by Victoria Cooper

Edited by Limitless Creations

Chapter 1

Escape plan

"Leave it alone! You'll make it explode again." Sage's tone verged on grumpy, even though she'd just had an hour-long nose-to-tail massage and was splayed on her belly on the most comfortable cushion known to cat-kind.

Archie, my favorite giant hellhound, whined. "It didn't explode the last time I touched it."

"I barely escaped with my life when those fiery bubbles spat at me. It's your magic. Come away from it if you can't control your power." Sage hissed a warning.

I left the cooling cucumber slices over my eyes as Sage and Archie continued to bicker. I didn't need to remove them to know what Archie was playing with. The luxury spa retreat I'd brought us to was built over a volcanic lava flow, which heated the pools and saunas. It also meant there were occasional explosions of intensely hot magma. And Archie, being an impulsive hellhound, was drawn to the heat and kept toying with it. The last time he'd done so, he'd almost burned down the cocktail bar while Sage was in there, enjoying a double-cream cocktail with a large plate of plump pink shrimp.

"Isn't it time for your glossing treatment?" I murmured as I lounged on a ridiculously soft bed, dappled sunlight warming me.

"Archie should have been in the treatment room five minutes ago," Sage said. "He's late for everything."

"I thought you'd booked in at the same time as Sammy?" I asked. "He'll be wondering where you are."

"I want to play," Archie said, the hint of a whine in his words. "And my fur's shiny enough already."

"You look like a mangy mop, despite all your treatments," Sage said. "Go and get glossed and give us some peace."

Archie huffed out a sigh before the pad of his large paws revealed he was on his way to the treatment rooms.

I'd brought some of my magical misfits away on a two-week, all-expenses-paid, spa vacation. My charming Sammy was also here. After everything we'd recently gone through in Crimson Cove, we deserved a break with minimal drama.

And as much as I was missing my wonderful witch, Zandra Crypt, the time away gave me a chance to reflect on things. Mainly, my life choices, and what I should do about my twisty future.

"I'll order salmon mousse cupcakes," Sage said. "I can't get enough of those things."

"That's your third plate today," I said. "But why not? We're here to relax and enjoy ourselves."

Sage nudged a cucumber slice off my eye. "You don't seem relaxed."

"I'm blissed out. I couldn't be more at peace," I said.

"The masseuse said how tense you were."

"Which is why we're here. We've been through trying times, so we deserve this."

There was a shriek from inside the spa, a crash, and a few seconds later, Archie bounded out, swiftly followed by Sammy, who dripped a musky-scented oil onto the marble tiles.

"That wasn't my fault!" Archie cowered against the wall. "I didn't see the burner full of oil. And I didn't mean to knock it over."

"What have you done now?" Sage asked. "If you're not careful, they'll throw us out, and we have two days left. I'm not missing the all-you-can-eat steak tartare evening for anything."

"He didn't mean to bump into the oil burner." Sammy sniffed the goop on his fur. "He got excited when the spa lady rubbed his belly, and he wagged his tail too fast."

"This vacation was supposed to chill you out! It's made you even worse than usual." Sage flopped onto her belly again.

I flipped the other cucumber slice off my eye, rolled off the couch, and did a big stretch. "I'll smooth things over." I left Sage reprimanding Archie and headed inside the spa. The place was full of magic, and the staff were adept at clearing up any mess with an impressive efficiency. By the time I'd gotten to the treatment room to assess the damage, everything looked normal.

I'd tipped the staff generously when we arrived and cautioned them about Archie's rambunctious nature. But they took it all in their stride. The spa's employees had wonderfully calm auras, floating around without a care in the world. An overexcitable giant hellhound who occasionally set fire to things didn't faze them.

I returned to my friends to find a platter of salmon mousse cupcakes, steak strips marinated in butter, and some of Sammy's favorite chicken strips had arrived. We set about the food, commenting on how excellent it was. The whole spa was excellent. This had been a perfect idea.

Sammy tossed back a salmon cupcake. He was about to take another when Sage nudged him. He glanced at me and looked away.

Sage nudged him again.

"Is there something on your mind?" I asked Sammy.

He gulped. "Although we appreciate you bringing us here, Juno, we've... well, we've been talking. And we're worried about you."

"What, in particular, is worrying you?" I gobbled down a buttery strip of steak.

"You've never been away from Zandra for this long," Sage said. "You must be missing her."

"I am."

"I miss Vorana, but I contact her several times a day, so I know what's going on back home. You've only briefly messaged Zandra twice since we've been here."

"My witch needs a break, too." I bit into a chicken strip, deliberately not looking at my friends.

Sammy twitched his tail. "Juno, we're all worried. It isn't like you to avoid Zandra."

I finally glanced at my group of friends and witnessed the worry in their eyes. "Don't be. Everything is good in the world."

"Then why aren't you talking to Zandra?" Sage asked.

"I call Remus every night," Archie said. "And I even zapped myself home to see him one evening because I missed him too badly."

"I'm glad you have such strong bonds," I said. "But I don't need to be in touch with Zandra to know all is well. If she were in trouble, I'd know about it."

"It's not that." Sage paused. "We know why you arranged this vacation so quickly."

"Crimson Cove has been hectic, and we all needed a time out. We barely survived Christmas because there was a demon hiding among us. Angel Force is still getting over that embarrassment," I said.

"And Zandra is still getting over you using magic to make her forget something important," Sage said. "I know she wants to talk to you about it."

"Oh, that! I'd quite forgotten. Do you want any more of the cupcakes?" I wasn't discussing the use of a memory suppress spell on my witch.

"You need to sort this," Sage said. "We all agree. Keeping secrets from your bonded magic user is wrong."

"Gossip less about me and focus on yourselves," I said. "My relationship with Zandra is perfect."

Archie whimpered softly. "We don't mean to upset you, but we think it's important."

"I'm not upset." I pushed away my last piece of steak.

"Zandra knows you're different. So do we. We still like you," Archie said.

"We're all a little different," I said. "That's why we're magical misfits. There's no shame in that."

"Yet you're the only misfit hiding a giant secret from your bonded witch," Sage said. "She's already had a taste of your power and handled it. Stop skirting the issue. Zandra's been around powerful magic most of her life. What you've got won't be a problem for her."

"You don't know that for certain," I said. "Why change things when they work just as they are?"

"It's not working, though, is it?" Sage nudged Sammy. "You agree, don't you?"

Sammy choked on his piece of chicken before swallowing. "I want you and Zandra to be happy. Your bond will be stronger if you're honest with each other."

"We're both happy," I said.

"If you're so blissed out, then why are you ignoring Zandra?" Sammy asked. "I don't have anyone I'm bonded to, but if I did, I'd never let them out of my sight. It must feel strange not being around Zandra for such a long time."

I had to admit, it felt less than ideal, but I needed time to figure out an action plan. Zandra knew my magic was unusual. I'd given her a tiny taste of it to keep her alive during a particularly vicious battle, but she'd only had the briefest of tastes. She didn't know what I really was. When she did, I couldn't be certain she'd want me around.

"You need to tell her the truth," Sage said. "We can help you figure out a way to do it."

"That's not an option," I said. "At least, not yet."

"Would you be willing to give up your magic?" Sammy asked. "There are those magic carriers who do. Some people never take to magic. You could even channel it into someone else, so you didn't have to suppress all that energy."

"No one would survive such power." I didn't mean to sound arrogant, but it was simply the truth. Ancient demigoddess magic could only be contained by a few immensely powerful individuals. If anyone took all my power, it would consume them until they were nothing more than a shattered, ashy husk, drifting in the breeze.

"Use a vessel," Sammy said. "A containment jar. Something that would hold your magic."

"What would I be then?" I asked. "Your average cat?"

"Even your average cat is awesome," Archie said. "They always stand up to me when I chase them. I respect that."

I shook my head. "With no magic, I'd be unable to protect Zandra. That is unacceptable."

"Could you put part of it in a container and keep the rest? Would that work?" Sammy asked.

"The magic would become unstable," I said. "I wouldn't be able to choose what kind of magic I kept. And since we often find ourselves dealing with unscrupulous types and facing danger, I can't make myself vulnerable. How would I keep Zandra safe with a patchwork of spells and powers?"

Sage sighed. "Then change Zandra. Channel more of your magic into her. You can both be fancy-pants goddesses together and lord it over us."

"I've never explicitly told you that's what I am," I said.

"You reek of entitlement and ancient power," Sage said. "It's got to be something like that. But like the others, I don't care. We're your friends. You could grow an extra head and lose your tail again, and I'd still put up with you."

Sammy nodded. "We know you're unique. You're special to us."

Archie wagged his tail in agreement. He couldn't talk because his mouth contained half a cow.

My gaze shifted to the stunning magma flow that oozed down a nearby mountain. Hot, bright sparks and occasional flares burst from the molten heat. I'd come away to avoid pressure, not be whacked around the head with it. My friends meant well, but they didn't fully understand my situation.

I'd controlled realms, wielded powerful magic with the blink of an eye, and had thousands of adoring subjects. Where did my modern life fit with my old one? I couldn't see a way to squeeze the two together and make a comfortable fit.

But now Zandra knew I'd been hiding things, and with my friends badgering me, I had to do something.

There was another crash from inside the spa. I looked over, half-expecting to see Archie had disappeared, but he was still happily chewing on his cow strips.

A few seconds later, the three sprightly black kittens I'd taken under my paw bundled onto the pagoda, play-fighting with each other. They were a welcome distraction from my interrogation.

"No! No kittens ruining our day. They should be in daycare until dinner time." Sage lowered her ears, her gaze narrowing as the kittens rolled too close to her.

"They must have broken free." I'd had to bring the kittens with us. Sorcha Creer had agreed to take them back and look after them at the café, but she returned them a few days later, saying they were too powerful, and she was worried the building would burn down the second her back was turned.

I'd been unable to find anyone else to take them at such short notice, and Sage had refused to have them in Vorana's house while we were away. That meant they had to come with us. The spa had been accommodating and had excellent facilities for magical youngsters.

And most of the time, the kittens behaved themselves, but there had been several breakouts from daycare and a few tiny fires.

"When will you find a proper home for these troublemakers?" Sage hissed as a kitten rolled too close and batted at her tail.

"Their power is unique. I need to keep them close until I figure out what to do with them," I said. "And you refused to let me leave them with Zandra and Vorana, so this was the only option."

"They're out of control! They're mini menaces." Sage swiped at another kitten.

Archie grabbed a kitten in his giant mouth and settled it on his back. "They're adorable. And their magic is something else. Maybe they're hell kittens. Is that a thing? You get hellhounds, so why not hell cats?"

"It's something I'm investigating," I said. "For now, they stay with me. It's the safest place for them. And for everyone else."

Two of the daycare staff rushed out wearing fireproof outfits, holding toys with feathers and small bells as they chased the kittens around, rounding them up as they leaped, hissed, twirled, and caused mayhem.

"You see, everything is under control," I said.

Archie stamped out a few small fires caused by the kittens before settling in to finish his steak.

"I'm sorry to bother you." A smartly dressed receptionist, who smelled faintly of incense and honey, appeared in the doorway. "There are messages for you, Juno."

I got up and followed her back to the reception desk. There was one call from Zandra I'd missed, checking in to see how I was doing. The next set of messages were more alarming: six calls from Granny Dottie in Willow Tree Falls and twenty messages from Wiggles, Tempest Crypt's mini hellhound sidekick. Why were the Crypt witches contacting me here? How did they know I was here?

The Crypt witches were a self-contained coven, immensely powerful, and specialists in trapping and imprisoning the worst kind of demon. There must be trouble in their village if they were reaching out to me.

I yelped as the kittens landed on my back and dug in their tiny claws. I rolled over several times to dislodge them, but they saw it as a game and clung on tighter. All of them smoked, suggesting they were building up a huge ball of flames.

"Archie! I need your help!"

He bounded into the reception area.

"Sit on these kittens," I instructed. "Don't let them get away."

He swiped the kittens off me with a giant paw then lay on his belly, the protesting kittens squirming beneath him with no hope of getting free until he decided otherwise.

"Stay there until you learn how to behave," I said. Archie could easily handle the kittens' tiny fireballs as they protested and smoked beneath him. They most likely felt like miniature hot water bottles to a fine hellhound specimen like Archie.

I looked at the messages again. Granny Dottie's were basically the same: *Have fun at the spa but call as soon as you can. There's trouble brewing.*

What trouble was too much for the Crypt witches to deal with?

Wiggles' messages were increasingly desperate: *Call me. Where are you? Emergency. Emergency. Emergency. Are you alive? Help!*

Something terrible had panicked him. I started with Wiggles and used the magic snow globe on the reception desk to connect a call.

Wiggles' damp brown nose loomed on the globe, and his breath fogged the glass.

"Greetings, Wiggles. What's going on?" I asked. "I just collected all of your messages."

He wheezed out a breath. "Zandra said you'd gone away without her."

"I'm at a spa with friends. What's wrong?"

He stepped back, and I could clearly see from his panting and twitching that all was far from well.

"I need your help," he said. "It's Tempest. She's missing."

Chapter 2

Lost witch

"Everyone is listening. Tell us what's going on." After Wiggles' panicked revelation that one of Willow Tree Falls' most powerful residents had gone AWOL, I'd gathered my friends so we could learn more and come up with a plan.

"Tempest has been missing since yesterday," Wiggles said.

"It's not unusual for her to leave the village when she's working," I said. "She gets sent on missions by Angel Force to locate misbehaving demons from all magical realms."

"Sure. But it's not work related! She's done no work for days."

"Maybe Tempest needed to recharge somewhere peaceful," Sage said. "It's what we're doing."

"Not without me! What kind of cupcakes have you got there? They look pink. Are they sweet or savory?" Wiggles asked.

"Salmon. They're delicious," I said.

"I'm too stressed to eat, even though they look good. Send me some, in case I change my mind," Wiggles said. "What should I do about Tempest?"

"Have you checked in with your local branch of Angel Force?" I asked. "They could have sent her on a covert mission."

"If she does anything covert, I'm always there," Wiggles said.

"Not if it's outside Willow Tree Falls. Your magic doesn't allow it. Where have you searched?"

"Everywhere! I've looked all over."

"The club?"

"Yes!"

"Tempest could be spending a romantic day or two with Rhett," I said.

"I've been to his house. She's not with him. At first, he wasn't worried, but when Tempest didn't show, and Rhett couldn't get hold of her, he got anxious. He even got his old biker friends to roam around looking for her. They drew a blank."

Rhett Blackthorn was Tempest's significant other. He was a fallen angel with a degree of power and used to run with a rough crowd, but he'd reformed since coupling with Tempest.

"What else is Rhett doing to find Tempest?" I asked.

"The same as me, but it's getting us nowhere," Wiggles said. "And I can't leave Willow Tree Falls without the right magic in place, so I'm stuck looking around here."

"You're really that concerned that you want to leave the village?" I asked.

"Something feels wrong." Wiggles hesitated and blew out smoke. "And it's not just Tempest's disappearance that's worrying me. Things are strange in Willow Tree Falls. There's a funky atmosphere."

"A funky atmosphere that could have whisked away your witch?" I asked.

"Imagine the power it would take to defeat a Crypt witch," Sage muttered. "Tempest wouldn't go down without an enormous, vicious, blood-spattered fight."

"Exactly! If something's gotten a hold of Tempest, it won't mess around." Wiggles huffed, smoke obscuring him for a second. "I've got to find her. I'm so worried that my stomach's upset. I've got so much gas I'm gonna float away."

"No one wants to be around a hellhound with an irritable bowel," I said. "What do you need us to do?"

"Help with the search. You can go wherever you like."

"I'm happy to," I said. "Zandra left me a message, so you must have been in contact with her, too."

"She told me I was overreacting, just like you. But we know when there's something wrong with our witches, don't we? It's like a tiny bit of me is missing. It's not as bad as when you lost your entire tail and had to walk around looking like a fluffy white marshmallow for months, but it feels as if something's gone. And I must get it back."

"Tell us more about the weirdness in your village," Sage said. "If there's something troubling the whole village, it may be Tempest isn't the only one at risk."

15

"She's not at risk," I said hurriedly, not wanting to panic Wiggles. "We don't know for certain anything has happened to her. And if anything or anyone has taken Tempest, they'll regret it. She lets no one fool with her. Go on, Wiggles, what else is happening?"

"Our stone circle is chucking its toys out of the pram," Wiggles said.

"What's so special about a stone circle?" Archie asked.

"It's our village's guardian. It absorbs magic and gives it out. Tempest recharges from it when she's been using a ton of spells. The last time I went to the stones, they were cold and silent. It's as if the magic's been sucked out of them."

"No magical being should be able to affect your stones," I said. "They've stood upright for millennia, pulsing with ancient power."

"They're not pulsing now," Wiggles said. "I even risked peeing on one, and nothing happened. Normally, I get zapped with a warning to be more respectful. I'm telling you, if our stones are being messed with, then we're all in trouble. There's something in the air. It's that crackly kind of tension. Everyone's feeling it. They're snapping at each other or acting odd."

"We'll make a plan and get back to you as soon as we can," I said. "In the meantime, do nothing foolish."

"I'll do whatever it takes to get Tempest back," Wiggles said. "If I have to wear a clown nose and streak naked through the village, I'll do it!"

We ended our call and settled around fresh snacks that had been delivered by a thoughtful employee.

"Does the tiny hound usually overreact like that?" Archie asked.

"Wiggles is a freewheeling hellhound. It takes a lot to unsettle him," I said. "We should take this seriously, especially if Tempest has really vanished."

"What if someone has sucked the magic out of their standing stones?" Sammy asked. "What does it mean for Willow Tree Falls?"

"It would mean the village is magically dead," I said. "Magic users need a primal source to recharge. Crimson Cove has ley lines, and Willow Tree Falls has the ancient standing stones. It's not possible to remove the magic from them, though. The stones wouldn't allow it."

"Never say never," Sage mumbled around a mouthful of salmon cupcake. "I suppose you want our help to fix this muddle?"

"I do. We'll start with location spells," I said. "If we're all flinging them out, it'll be easier to find her. We'll begin with our searching magic focused on Willow Tree Falls and work our way out. That area is full of small magical villages, though, so it'll take time. It's a lot of power to sift through."

"We'll finish these cupcakes first, though, right?" Sage asked. "We need to be fully fueled before doing this."

"You can cast spells and eat at the same time," I said.

"I'll start," Sammy said. "My belly is full."

The magical snow globe we'd borrowed from the reception desk pinged with an incoming message. It was Wiggles again.

I opened it.

"Tempest is back! She strolled through the door a minute ago as if nothing odd had happened. Look, see for yourself." He shoved the globe with a paw to reveal Tempest sitting next to him.

Tempest's mildly annoyed expression hinted at her embarrassment at being the center of attention. "Hey, Juno. What's Wiggles been saying about me?"

"Greetings! Wiggles has been worried," I said. "Where have you been?"

"None of your beeswax. I was nowhere. See you later." Tempest cut the call abruptly.

"The tiny hound was worrying about nothing?" Archie asked.

"Talk about a drama pup," Sage said.

"Wiggles is a strange creature, but I'm concerned about how quiet their village's standing stones are," I said. "If things don't turn around, we'll take a trip to Willow Tree Falls to make sure nothing is wrong."

"Does this mean we can go back to eating, getting massaged, and sleeping?" Sage asked.

"In a minute. I'll call Zandra and give her the news about Tempest. She'll be concerned about her sister."

"And will you address the giant pink sparkly dragon in the corner of the room while you're talking?" Sage asked.

"I see no dragon, so there's no need to address it." I returned the snow globe to the reception desk, so I'd have privacy as I spoke to Zandra. I didn't want

Sage dropping unsubtle hints in the background while we talked.

It took a few seconds to connect, but Zandra appeared.

"Hey! I figured you'd forgotten about me. Still having fun?" she asked.

"We were having a most relaxing time until Wiggles got in touch."

"Sorry about that. He wouldn't stop pestering me until I gave him the details of the spa," Zandra said.

"Do you know Tempest is missing?"

"Wiggles told me. He's worrying about nothing," Zandra said. "I bet she's already back."

"She just showed up. Wiggles was relieved."

"He's been possessive ever since the kittens latched onto Tempest," Zandra said. "She told me they keep visiting Willow Tree Falls and attacking Wiggles."

"The kittens grew fond of Tempest when she stayed with us, but I didn't realize they'd been to Willow Tree Falls. They're sneaky."

"Uh-huh." Zandra nodded and glanced away.

"Are you busy with work?"

"Not so much. Randal's got friends in town. Tech mages, too. He's bringing them into animal control every day, and they've been tinkering with odd bits of equipment. They're here now, and something just exploded."

"Do they work for animal control, too?" I asked.

"No, although they do freelance on the side of their regular jobs. Randal said they had some downtime, so he invited them to stay. Erick and Charlie. You'll meet them when you get back."

"Zandra, come take a look at this!" Randal's voice sounded in the background.

She sighed. "They want to show me another odd gadget I'll have no clue what to do with. Gotta go. Have fun."

I said goodbye, but she'd already hung up. Zandra had seemed surprisingly unconcerned about Tempest's disappearing act. And she'd been so quick to end the call that I hadn't had a chance to tell her about the problems in Willow Tree Falls. Wiggles must have mentioned them, so why wasn't she more concerned?

"Zandra's coldness is your fault."

I jumped at the sound of Sage's voice behind me and pivoted to face her. "Don't creep up on me like that. I may be powerful, but I'm also ancient."

"You forgot to add annoying to your list of unique qualities."

I hissed softly at her.

"Zandra was off with you." Sage ambled over, her back harness wheels squeaking slightly.

"Untrue! Zandra was distracted by Randal blowing something up. I'm happy she's got him keeping her company."

"She was offhand because she knows you're still keeping secrets. You can only paw step around the truth for so long before it becomes an issue. Once it gets too big, you've got real problems. These Crypt witches hold grudges."

"You don't know them well enough to say that," I said.

"Mark my words, the longer you keep a secret, the harder it'll bite you in the behind," Sage said.

"Nonsense. Let's get back to those salmon cupcakes."

"I ate them. We can always order more. And didn't Wiggles want you to send him some? Get a double batch, just in case I'm hungry later."

After requesting a box of cupcakes be dispatched to Willow Tree Falls and another plate for us, I sighed as I returned to the pagoda with Sage.

Perhaps it was time to get back to Crimson Cove and face the music.

⁂

The last two days at the spa passed uneventfully. The kittens only started half a dozen fires, and Archie knocked over only two things—and one of those didn't break—so we left with success following us.

Even though I'd been pummeled, massaged, and had my paws cleansed, tension crept along my spine as I stood outside the house with Sage and my foster kittens. We'd said goodbye to the others, and they'd gone home.

"Let's get inside," Sage said. "I can't wait to see Vorana."

I took a deep breath. I wanted to see Zandra and figure things out. Our bond was stronger than any problem.

Sage charged ahead, and by the time I'd gotten into the kitchen, she was out of her harness and settled in the papoose Vorana Stowell had wrapped around her middle. Vorana stood by the stove, a big smile on her face as she cooed to Sage, who purred and made air biscuits with her paws.

"Welcome home," Vorana said when she saw me. "I've planned a feast to celebrate your return. Six courses!"

"Sounds positively medieval," I said. "Count me in. Where's Zandra?"

"Not back from work," Vorana said. "She's been staying late recently."

"Has animal control been busy while I've been away?" After cautioning the kittens to behave, I hopped onto my usual chair and settled my paws on the wooden table in the kitchen. It felt good to be home.

"She hasn't mentioned it being busy. Randal has a couple of friends staying, though, so she's been going out with them."

If I'd had eyebrows, I'd have raised them. "How interesting."

"They're having fun. Zandra even mentioned Randal's been making her laugh. I get the impression Randal's friends are bringing him out of his shell. He seems more confident," Vorana said.

"Excellent. I sense progress with their relationship," I said. "I'd almost given up hope Zandra and Randal would ever get together."

Vorana chuckled. "They're not together, but they are spending much more time with each other. They've been going to the bar next to the workshop if you want to find her."

I nodded my thanks and left Vorana and Sage together in their bonded bliss. After tucking the kittens in for a nap, I decided to walk to the bar.

It was a fair distance, but after two weeks of doing nothing but lounging around and feasting, I needed exercise to work off the small roll of salmon mousse cupcakes that had settled around my middle.

As I wandered, I was happy to see Crimson Cove was much the same. People bustled home from work. The early dining crowd was heading to the pizza parlor and cafes, and everything felt good. Normal. Just how I wanted it to remain. Why throw a magical hand grenade into such a peaceful situation when there was no need?

I arrived at the bar. It was quiet, with the seasoned drinkers yet to take up residence, so it was easy to find Zandra, Randal, and his friends. They occupied a booth, and there was a scattering of mechanical objects across their table. Tech mages love their toys.

I tugged on my bond to let Zandra know I was there, and she turned, raising a hand when she saw me. I leapt onto her lap and accepted some back scratches.

"Your fur is so silky," Zandra said. "And you smell like flowers. Is that honeysuckle?"

"The spa was most invigorating," I said. "Greetings, Randal."

"Hey! Juno. Meet Charlie Victor and Erick Farten."

I nodded at the newcomers. Charlie was short and well-muscled, with virtually no neck and a large, bushy ginger beard. His eyebrows matched his beard, and his eyes were a sparkling blue.

Erick was leaner, clean-shaven, with a nose that had a moist tip, and dull green eyes. They were around the same age as Zandra and Randal and wore a relaxed style of clothing, much like Randal—sneakers, jeans, and long-sleeved T-shirts.

"What have we got going on here?" I lightly batted a loose piece of metal that had rolled across the table.

"We've been dazzling Zandra with our inventions." Erick leered at Zandra and made a grab for her arm. He sniffed up a small trail of nose drippage. "Although she's yet to see the benefits of having three powerful tech mages to do her bidding."

"If you were doing my bidding, I'd have an endless supply of beers and burgers coming my way." Zandra less than discreetly leaned away from Erick. "You've been so distracted with your gadgets that we haven't even ordered."

"Save your appetite for when we get home," I said. "Vorana is planning a feast."

"Oh, yeah. She mentioned that," Zandra said. "I'll just have a side of fries with my beer."

"I'll go to the bar. They seem short-staffed this evening." Randal got everyone's order and dashed away.

I leaned against Zandra's belly. So far, so comfortable. Zandra was acting normally, and it looked like I'd been given a pass for the evening. Maybe we wouldn't need to have our awkward conversation just yet.

A scream rang out from the other side of the bar, and I leapt up, my hackles lifted. My foster kittens bounced from table to table, setting fire to anything remotely flammable then dancing away with magic sparkling around them. "What are they doing here? I put them down for a nap when I got back to Vorana's."

"They don't want to be without you," Zandra said. "They must've gotten attached."

"I'll round them up and send them home." I raced off and corralled the misbehaving kittens with firm words and several powerful spells.

They were a magical handful, and it took me twenty minutes to get all three under control and safely magicked to Vorana's house.

Once they were tucked in again in their cozy bed in the warmest part of the basement, I sat back and gave them my sternest glare until they fell silent and stared at me. "If I see any more naughtiness tonight, you'll get no supper. And no outdoor playtime tomorrow. I'm not messing about. You've just come back from a lovely vacation, so don't spoil it. Go to sleep. You're tired."

The kittens seemed to have had enough adventuring, or maybe they really thought I would punish them. They curled into a giant bundle of fur, yawning and closing their eyes.

Despite being so badly behaved, they were adorable little bundles of magical fluff. What to do with those powerful tiny fluff balls was a mystery I'd yet to figure out.

To save time, I translocated back to the bar. I was about to open the door when a chair crashed through the window.

Chapter 3

World war witch

Splintered glass landed on the ground in a sharp arc that would punish my toe beans if I wasn't careful. I slammed open the door to discover chaos. Tables were overturned, people were shouting, and a thick haze of smoke hovered in the air.

I stayed low as I surveyed the mayhem. Randal was at the center, tangled up with a burly witch who had him in a headlock. His face was red as he fumbled for something in his pocket. Whatever it was, he couldn't reach it.

I darted closer, dodging a broken bottle as it spun across the floor. Randal's eyes caught mine, wide and a little desperate.

Zandra was backed into a corner, her hands crackling with magical energy. She shot a quick burst of light at an advancing figure, sending him stumbling back, dazed and blinking.

"This wasn't how I planned on spending my evening!" she yelled, throwing a brief grin my way. My witch enjoyed testing her power, but what had happened in my absence to cause such bedlam?

Before I could move, a man with fists like bricks lunged toward me, swinging with wild, unfocused rage. I ducked and lunged, raking my claws across his thigh, watching him stumble back with a grunt. He clutched his leg, eyes blazing as he reached into his pocket, pulling out a sparking wand. A blast of magic shot in my direction. I darted sideways, feeling heat graze past my ear.

Randal finally wrestled free of his attacker, breathing hard. "Could you handle her, Juno? I'm useless without my tech, and everything we have here is experimental."

"You should be experimenting your tech on these people! They're out of control." I moved in, ready to pounce if the witch made any devious plays.

Across the room, I spotted Erick huddled under a table, clutching a piece of tech like it was a life raft. I couldn't decide if he was fiddling with it or praying to it, but either way, he was as good as useless. One of the bar brawlers—a wiry woman with a busted lip and a gleam in her eye—spotted him and advanced.

With a growl, I leapt across the room and planted myself between them, hissing loud enough that she took a step back. Her eyes narrowed, and I could see her sizing me up, debating whether to take me on or go after easier prey. In the end, she sneered and backed off.

"Th-thanks, Juno," Erick stammered, his knuckles white around his gadget.

"Help your friends!" I shot him a look and darted back into the fray.

Zandra was holding her own, though she was cornered by two witches who must be using a spell-nullifying talisman. Her usual bursts of magic sputtered against it, leaving her only with sheer will and brute force. Fortunately, she had plenty of both.

Just as one witch lunged, I dashed between them, swiping at her legs with my murder mittens, my magic sparking. She dodged away, giving Zandra time to sidestep the danger.

Randal was evading punches and magic blasts from two sides, his tech misfiring as he aimed it. He gritted his teeth, slapped the side of his device, and muttered, "Come on, work!"

A weak spark shot out of the gadget, hitting his nearest opponent in the shoulder. It didn't do much. Just enough for the man to look confused and maybe a little insulted.

"Randal, ditch the tech and fight! You know spells." I darted back as a chair swung through the air, narrowly missing my head.

He grunted, tossing the device aside and balling his fists. He threw a sparking punch that landed on his opponent's jaw, sending him staggering backward. Randal glanced down at his hand, wincing.

A grim-faced elderly man lunged at me from the side, and I barely had time to react. Why was everyone throwing out punches and spells like this was a purge day?

With a swift flick of my murder mittens, I extended my claws and shot out a spell. He hissed in pain as it landed, backing off long enough for me to regroup.

My heart skittered. Zandra was surrounded. Her hands sparked as she conjured a barrier, but I could tell she was getting worn down. My witch needed help.

I advanced on the attackers. With a low growl, I focused my energy, and a shield shimmered into being.

"What happened to start this?" I yelled.

"No clue! A fight erupted out of nowhere." Zandra's attention was fixed on her attackers. "One moment, we were nursing our drinks, and the next, chaos stirred to life. And I don't think we're done yet. Help Randal's buddies. I've got this under control."

Erick and Charlie stood together, fumbling with their tech gadgets. Judging by the awkward clinking and beeping sounds, I wasn't optimistic about their reliability.

Charlie jabbed at a device, and a puff of glittering smoke erupted from it, blinding him.

"Incoming!" Zandra had a hand raised. She flung her palm forward, and a shimmering force pushed two witches back, slamming them into a nearby table. Bottles and glasses shattered on impact, and the scent of beer filled the air.

Randal was still swinging sparking punches but was knocked off his feet by a guy twice his size. "Now would be a great time to join in, Erick!" He glared at his blundering friend, who was still fiddling with his tech, which emitted a low, sputtering whine.

Erick finally got a gadget working—sort of. A tiny sphere shot out, ricocheting across the room before exploding in a burst of harmless sparks. It illuminated the bar with a brief, dazzling flash, giving Zandra and me a clear view of the remaining fighters. It also lit him up like a firework, and he got whacked by a barstool.

Erick staggered, eyes wide, blinking like he couldn't believe he'd been hit. He ducked behind an overturned table, clutching at his head. He peered over the edge of the table then cowered when a glass bottle went sailing past.

"Erick, do something useful!" Randal shouted, blocking a spell from another fighter.

Erick held up his gadget. "Uh, what do you want me to do? It's malfunctioning! You were supposed to help me fix this thing."

One of the brawlers spotted Erick cowering and made a beeline for him, a wicked grin spreading across his face. I darted across the room and positioned myself between them, letting out a low, menacing snarl.

The man hesitated, glancing from me to Erick. Doubt flickered in his eyes before he backed off, deciding he wasn't up for a fight with a magical, furious feline.

"Thanks, Juno," Erick mumbled. "I'm so scared, I could puke."

"Avoid that at all costs." I looked around the chaos. There were still a few angry looking people, their fists clenched and eyes narrowed, magic sparkling around them, but the desire to destroy had faded as fast as it had begun. Everyone seemed confused as they staggered away or helped friends up.

I looked at Zandra as she ran over. "This is what happens when I leave you on your own?"

She lifted one shoulder. "Not my fault."

Randal nodded as he joined us. "It's as if someone lit a fuse, and everybody else got dragged into the fight."

"It was fight or die." Charlie inspected a tear in his jacket as he walked over. "And I'm not known for my fighting prowess."

"Without my gadgets, I'm useless," Randal said.

"Erick, that head wound looks nasty," I said. "Let me heal it for you."

He shuffled out from his hiding place and crouched in front of me, staying on his knees. "Could Zandra do it?"

I huffed out a breath. "Zandra is exhausted."

She shrugged. "I can handle a healing spell."

Erick's eyes lit up as he wiped his nose on the back of his hand.

Zandra stepped away. "But you do it, Juno."

Erick frowned but accepted my help. "Defence and attack spells escape me. I never could figure them out."

"We noticed." Zandra cast a look around the bar to ensure no one wanted to try their luck with us.

"I did my best!" Erick's bottom lip jutted out. "I once invented a machine that printed plasters you could fill with healing magic. They were custom printed to fit the size of the wound. The problem was you needed a proficient magic user standing beside the machine to make it work."

"You basically invented a plaster maker," I said.

Randal chuckled as he nodded.

"Not true! I've also been working on getting it to shrink so it can be a portable gadget." Erick winced as I sparked my magic. "Although, so far, the results haven't been promising."

"You're a big ideas guy," Randal said. "We all are. We need someone in the group who can finish the projects we dream up."

"It's a sensible idea." I gently rested my paws on Erick's sweaty head, close to the wound, to heal him. "We all have strengths we can play to, and it's not a failing to admit you're weak in an area."

"You're an amazing fighter," Erick said to Zandra. "You were blasting out spells like they were nothing more than sneezes."

"I've never had my magic compared to a sneeze," Zandra said. "Should I say thanks or bless you?"

"Oh! It was a compliment. You were incredible. You lifted your hands, and this power poured out. It was hot," Erick said.

Zandra shook out her hands. "Yeah, it's been doing that lately." She glanced at me.

"Randal talks about you all the time," Erick continued. "He's so impressed by your talents. And I can see why."

Randal blushed. "Zandra is unique. She's got skills I can barely dream about."

"My wonderful witch is perfectly unique," I said. "You wouldn't want anybody else by your side when the chips are down."

"Yeah, that's enough talk of chips, or I'll get even hungrier," Zandra said. "We never did get to eat. How's the head, Erick?"

"If you hold my hand, I'll feel much better."

Zandra grimaced. "How about we get out of here before someone else starts a fight?"

"We should go back to mine," Randal said. "I've got snacks."

"Sounds good. I don't want to stay here any longer than we need to," Charlie said.

"I'm glad I'm only staying in town for another night," Erick said. "This has been such a weird welcome. I'm looking forward to getting back to my lair. No one is allowed through those doors unless they have the top-secret password."

"Lair? Password?" Charlie chuckled. "Anyone would think you're Batman."

"You've seen my lair. It's even underground!" Erick looked to Zandra for approval. "And I almost passed my driver's test the last time I took it, so I can soon get a batmobile. I already know the model I want."

We headed out of the bar, picking our way over broken glass and chairs until we got outside, Randal and his friends still discussing cars and secret lairs.

"You should come with us." Erick reached for Zandra's hand. "I've got more tech to show you. I brought a whole suitcase with me."

"A suitcase of projects you expect me to fix." Randal frowned at Erick. "Stop bothering Zandra."

"Thanks, but we'll pass." Zandra picked me up and held me against her chest, so I was a barrier, protecting her from Erick's clammy, unwanted, nose dripping charms.

"I figured it would be fun." Erick kicked the dirt until he was cajoled away by Randal and Charlie,

Randal shooting us a mouthed *sorry* as they walked away.

We called out a goodnight and headed home, tired and more than a little shocked by what had happened. That bar wasn't rough, although it could be rowdy at the weekend, but it was family friendly, and I'd never seen things get out of hand like that before.

"We should find the people who started the fight and make them sorry," I said. "Do you know who it was?"

Zandra shook her head. "Two guys started it, then everyone else piled in. I didn't recognize them. Maybe they're just passing through town."

"I'll tell them not to return," I said. "Crimson Cove doesn't need more troublemakers stirring things up. We've got enough of those already."

"And I'm holding one of them." Zandra shifted me onto her shoulder for the walk home.

When we arrived at Vorana's house, I paused at the front door and inhaled deeply. "There's somebody here."

"Vorana's got guests? Is it Brodie? I didn't think he was due back yet." Zandra paused, her hand on the doorknob.

I hurried in the second she opened the door to discover Zandra and Tempest's Granny Dottie sitting in Vorana's living room, the three black kittens nestled on her lap, purring and half asleep.

"Greetings! This is a wonderful surprise. And you're a miracle worker," I said.

"I already know that." Granny Dottie had colored her hair a striking shade of magenta. "What miracle have I performed this time?"

"The kittens never sleep."

She smiled as she gently stroked them. "They're cute, but I'm not here about the kittens. I'm here because we have a problem smashing into the family, and I need it stopped."

Zandra was right behind me. She strode over and hugged Granny Dottie. "I didn't know you were coming. What's wrong?"

"It's Tempest. She's behaving strangely," Granny Dottie said.

"Wiggles has already been in touch." I settled on the couch next to Zandra. "He thought she'd gone missing, but then she showed up."

Granny Dottie paused as Vorana appeared with a tray laden with cakes and mugs. Sage was snuggled in her favorite papoose, although she was wide awake and taking everything in.

"I heard you come in, so I brought extra." Vorana set down the tray and poured the drinks.

"Tell us what's going on," Zandra said to Granny Dottie. "I thought Wiggles was overreacting."

"At first, so did I," Granny Dottie said. "But Tempest keeps vanishing and then shrugging it off as if she's doing nothing out of the ordinary. I get it. She's young, enjoying life, and doesn't want to report back to her family. But she's got responsibilities in Willow Tree Falls. She can't keep disappearing."

"Tempest could be going through a rebellious phase," Zandra said. "And she's not far off middle-age. It could be her hormones."

"Don't be cheeky," Granny Dottie said. "If Tempest is middle-aged, then I've been in the ground and turned to dust for a hundred years."

"How out of character is her behavior?" I asked.

"Tempest acts as if she can't remember where she's been. She's vague when I ask questions. She sometimes goes on covert missions for Angel Force, but this is different. It's as if she has a secret, but she doesn't know what it is." Granny Dottie shoved half a cake into her mouth and chewed noisily.

"Are you concerned her demon is back?" I asked.

Granny Dottie paused from her chewing and swallowed. She looked at Zandra. "You and Aurora helped Tempest with that pesky demon she had trapped inside her. I checked with Aurora, and she's still holding her tiny piece of demon. Nothing's changed."

"Do you think something happened when Tempest and Wiggles visited us recently?" I asked. "Zandra smells the same to me. She grew more pungent after taking her own chunk of demon. I can still smell it, so she isn't the problem."

"I do not stink like a demon!" Zandra sniffed her hair.

"Only to my excellent booping snooter," I said.

"I'm open to all possibilities," Granny Dottie said. "Since Zandra also has a piece of Tempest's demon, I got to thinking it could have wriggled out and rejoined with Tempest. It would explain the odd behavior. When that demon had all its power, it

36

could take over. Tempest would wake and find herself in strange places after the scheming demon went on a sugar binge and caused chaos."

"I don't think that happened. I feel no different," Zandra said. "Is there a way to test me to make sure I still have the demon?"

"That's why I'm here," Granny Dottie said. "If we know what we're dealing with, we can fix things."

The air shimmered, and Rhett Blackthorn, Tempest's fallen angel boyfriend, appeared. His dark hair was tousled, there was a fresh bruise blooming on his cheek, and his jacket was torn.

He took a second to orientate himself then nodded a hello. "Sorry for dropping in unannounced, but this news can't wait."

"It's fine," Vorana said. "Dottie said you might stop by. Did you find Tempest?"

Rhett looked around the group, nodding again at me and Zandra. "I found her. But she escaped. She was so angry and surrounded by this weird energy. I've never felt anything like that from her before." He winced and wrapped an arm around his ribs.

"Did Tempest attack you?" I asked.

"It's nothing bad, but she refused to listen to me. I told her to come back to Willow Tree Falls. We all want to help her."

"What did she do to you?" Zandra asked.

"She blasted me off my feet, and I slammed into a tree. Then she blasted me some more just for the fun of it and vanished."

"Sit down," Vorana urged. "We can get your injuries fixed. Would you like tea?"

"Have you got anything stronger?" Rhett eased into a chair, stifling a groan as he did so.

"Of course. Juno, can you help heal Rhett?" Vorana asked before dashing out of the room to find a bottle of liquor and a glass.

I walked over to Rhett and inspected his injuries. "From that painful wheezing, you could have internal bleeding. I can patch you up, but you should go to our local hospital. They're very good."

"See what you can do. I don't want to waste time. Tempest is in trouble, and we've got to help her."

"We're right with you," Zandra said. "Tempest was fine when she was here over the holidays, though. She was her usual chilled-out self."

"We need to act fast," Granny Dottie said. "I love Tempest, but we must contain her. We've got to keep her safe. Then I want to test her to see if her demon's acting up and then figure out a way to fix it."

"Where did you find her?" I asked as I treated Rhett's injuries.

"She was far from Willow Tree Falls," Rhett said. "In some random magical community I've never heard of. I asked why she was there, but she didn't know. She said she was taking a break from her stifling family and her irritating boyfriend and to leave her alone. I asked why she hadn't told Wiggles where she was going, but Tempest shrugged it off. She said she didn't have to tell him everything, and it was none of his business. But you know those two. Whenever they can, they do everything together."

"Wiggles sounded distressed when he contacted us," I said. "I could tell he was worried."

"We're all worried," Granny Dottie said. "Tempest's actions make no sense. One minute, she seems rational, but it's as if a switch flicks, and she changes. It must be a possession."

"Who's powerful enough to possess a Crypt witch?" I asked.

"Her demon did," Granny Dottie said.

"Only for a short time," Zandra said. "And we tore his energy apart, so he shouldn't be strong enough to mess with her anymore. Who else?"

There was a heartbeat of silence. It was a tough question to answer.

I finished healing Rhett, and he nodded his thanks. "We need to locate her. If we can pin Tempest down, she'll be easier to catch."

"I found her with a location spell," Rhett said. "She didn't make it easy, though."

"I know my sister," Zandra said. "Wherever she's hiding, I'll find her. Let's get started."

Vorana fussed around some more, freshening drinks and checking on everyone before we settled in.

I snuggled close to Zandra. She didn't have to say a word, but she was worried. She hadn't always been close to Tempest. There'd been issues when she was younger, and Zandra dragged herself through growing pains by using advanced magic when she was too young, but they now adored each other, and she was hurting because Tempest was in trouble.

"We'll find Tempest and make this right," I said softly.

"You bet we will." There was a steely resolve in Zandra's tone. Whatever it took, she was getting her sister back.

"Drink this." Granny Dottie passed a small glass full of brilliant green liquid to Zandra.

She inspected it. "Will this tell us if I still have Tempest's demon inside me?"

"If it's still there, you'll feel fine. If he's gone, then you'll need a bucket. A big one."

Vorana hurried off and brought back a bucket, which she passed to Zandra.

Zandra puffed out a breath then uncorked the vial and downed the liquid. Everyone held their breath, staring at her.

She burped. "That's a good sign, right? No puking means I still have the demon?"

"He's still there," Granny Dottie said on a sigh. "Which means he did nothing tricky when Tempest visited Crimson Cove. I don't understand! Her behavior is chaotic and unstable. She's acting like she did before you and Aurora helped her. If it's not a demon, what is doing this?"

"Let's find Tempest and ask her," I said. "If we all search, we'll find her quickly."

After Granny Dottie had eaten another slice of cake, we began casting location spells.

Zandra winced as sparks shot out of her hand and pinged around her. She stretched her fingers and shook out her hand.

"Is something wrong?" I asked.

"The spell doesn't want to work." She flexed her hands several times.

I focused on a mental image of Tempest and unleashed a location spell. Sparks shot out of me too and slammed into Rhett, making him yelp.

"Sorry! That magic wasn't meant for you," I said.

"What's wrong with the magic in this place?" Granny Dottie groused. "A simple location spell shouldn't misfire. Vorana, do you have the house warded?"

"There are protection spells but nothing that would do this to your magic," Vorana said.

"We're all tense," I said. "Let's take a moment to relax. We just came back from a bar fight, so our thoughts are scattered."

Granny Dottie arched a thin white eyebrow then flicked out her own location spell. It whizzed around the room, shattering several plates and making us duck.

"Whatever is doing this, it had better stop." Granny Dottie hoisted the kittens onto her shoulder and stood. Her power shimmered around her. "No one messes with my family and gets away with it."

"What if we joined our magic?" Rhett asked. "We pull on each other's power and form a link. That way, we won't be messed with. We'll be too powerful."

"Fallen angel power, Crypt witch magic, and whatever you've got going on there." Granny Dottie wiggled her fingers at me. "That will work."

"We can help, too," Vorana said. "Sage is powerful."

"I don't want you hurt by getting muddled in Crypt witch shenanigans," Sage said.

"It's just a location spell. We must help find Zandra's sister."

Sage grumbled some more but grudgingly joined the circle as everyone took a hand or a paw.

"Let's see where Tempest is hiding." Granny Dottie took the lead and thrust out the location magic.

Glass shattered, the ground shook as if an earthquake had just hit, and there was an enormous explosion.

⁕⁕⁕⁕⁕ ⁕⁕⁕⁕⁕

I woke on my back with my paws in the air to find Randal standing over me. I coughed and spluttered, rolling onto my side. I looked around, my vision blurry. Zandra was just rising, leaning over Granny Dottie.

"Juno, what happened?" Randal's face was pale, and his voice sounded strained. It looked like he'd been crying.

"We were looking for someone," I said. "How are you here?"

"I came to ask for help, but it looks like you need mine. Let me get you on your paws. Are you hurt?"

"I'm fine. See to Zandra. Make sure she's not injured," I said.

"She's good. I've already checked," he said. "Everyone's okay. No serious injuries."

I was grateful for that, but I was still shocked to the tip of my tail. Why had the world exploded when Granny Dottie threw out a location spell?

It took a few minutes before everyone was back on their feet and paws, looking stunned and with no explanations as to what happened. And three hours had passed! It was a shock to discover we'd all been out for such a long time.

I looked up at Randal. "You said you needed help?"

He gulped. "I... Yes. I don't know what to do. It's Erick, you see."

"Your friend? What about him?"

Tears filled Randal's eyes. "He's dead. And... Charlie is in a coma."

Chapter 4

Dead end

Shock and surprise overtook my confusion. "Randal, if you can find a seat that isn't broken, sit on it. I need a moment to process everything that's going on."

His knees wobbled as he sank onto a charred chair and ran a hand down his face. "I... I don't know what happened. I can't believe he's dead."

"Vorana, can you assist Randal?" I asked.

She had Sage in her arms, holding her close to her chest, her eyes wide with shock as she stared at the destroyed room. She nodded and gestured for me to go over to Zandra.

I raced over to check on my wonderful witch. It was a huge relief to find her unharmed, other than a smear of soot on her cheek.

"I'm good," she said. "You?"

"Unscorched, fortunately." I jumped onto her shoulder and snuggled against her neck. "What went wrong?"

Zandra looked around the room. Granny Dottie was dealing with several small fires that had erupted

44

after the spell backfired, being slowed down as the kittens bounced around her, unbothered by the explosion. Rhett was talking to Randal, who looked blank-faced with shock.

"I have no clue. Something felt wrong the second we activated the magic. But it makes no sense. I know everyone's magic here."

"Not so much Rhett's," I murmured. "I don't know him. He's a fallen angel. They can misbehave."

"Rhett's rough around the edges, but he's a good guy. And he adores Tempest. He'd do nothing to harm her."

"Even after she injured him so badly?" I whispered.

"They've been through worse struggles than this. It took him months to convince her he was serious about her, and even then, she held off. If Rhett wasn't dedicated to Tempest, he's had plenty of opportunities to bow out. I trust him."

"If you trust Rhett, so do I," I said. "But something in here smells fishy, and not the delicious, freshly cured kind."

All the fires were out, and Vorana had gotten Granny Dottie onto a comfortable beanbag. The kittens were on her lap again, purring as if nothing untoward had happened. We all gathered around Randal, who sat on the chair, his skin the color of spoiled milk, with dark smudges under his eyes.

"Tell us what happened to Erick," I said.

He gulped in air. "I don't know. After we met at the bar and got in that fight, we headed straight home."

"How did Erick seem when you got home?" I asked.

"The same as always. We talked about the bar fight, but none of us could figure out what triggered it. Charlie thought he saw two guys squaring off just before it broke out, but there were no raised voices. I saw nothing."

"Was Erick acting normally?" Zandra asked.

Randal nodded. "I got snacks and drinks, and we gamed for a while. It was a late session, and I crashed on the couch. When I woke, the room was freezing. All the windows and doors were open."

"You didn't open them?" I asked.

"No, I figured it was one of the other guys. I looked around, but they were gone."

"And that worried you?"

"Not initially. They have their own rooms, so I figured they crept up while I was sleeping or were getting more food from the kitchen. I looked around and saw no sign of them. I went up to their rooms. The beds hadn't been slept in. That was when I looked out the window."

"Erick was outside?" Zandra asked.

"I saw someone lying in the yard. I wasn't sure who it was. It was weird. Creepy. It's a full moon, so I could see it was a person," Randal said. "I headed down the stairs, grabbed my zapping device just in case, and went out the back. I found Charlie first. He was on the porch. I thought he was asleep, but I couldn't rouse him. Then I went to find Erick. That's when I knew something bad had gone down."

"Erick was dead when you found him?" Rhett asked.

Randal blinked several times. "His face was frozen in terror. His hands were in claws, as if he was digging his fingernails into something. He was just lying on the grass, staring at the sky, not seeing."

"I'm so sorry. That's awful," Zandra said.

"It's a messy business," Granny Dottie said. "Who do you think got him?"

Randal shook his head. "I've no clue. I didn't touch his body. Angel Force will need to check for evidence, but I saw no obvious wounds. I suppose they could have been on his back, but there was no blood. Nothing. It's as if he just died of fright."

"Which suggests magic," I said. "You mentioned Angel Force. Are they already at the scene?"

"No, I... I wasn't thinking straight," Randal said. "I was so panicked by finding Erick dead and Charlie in some kind of coma that I came straight here. I knew you'd help me." He looked around the destroyed room. "And I'm glad I did. Why were you all unconscious? Why was this place on fire?"

"Because Crimson Cove's magic is weird," Granny Dottie said. "I sensed it as soon as I arrived."

"Sorry, Randal, in all the chaos, I didn't introduce you. This is Zandra's Granny Dottie and Rhett Blackthorn. He's dating Zandra's older sister, Tempest," I said.

Randal just about managed a nod of greeting. "You think our town's magic is weird?"

"Something is wrong with it," Granny Dottie said.

"Could it be a spell you cast that caused this to happen?" Randal asked.

I winced. "Unlikely. Dottie is a powerful witch. A *Crypt* witch." Randal needed to be careful what toes he trod on. It was never smart to insult someone so powerful.

"And this Crypt witch doesn't like what you're suggesting, young man," Granny Dottie said.

"Oh. Sure. Sorry. But you must have powerful magic," Randal said. "Maybe you made a mistake. She looks old," he whispered to me.

"Old but with impeccable hearing, so be careful what you whisper next." A glimmer of magic twirled off Granny Dottie's hand.

Randal shrank back in his seat, and he mumbled an apology.

"They're here because Tempest is missing," I said. "We joined our powers to cast a more effective location spell. There was a hiccup."

"A hiccup suggests something small. This was more like one of Wiggles' more unpleasant gaseous rear end explosions. He can set a barn on fire if he stands the wrong way when he lets rip," Granny Dottie said. "My magic was working just fine until I got here. What's going on in this town? Have there been other problems like this?"

"Nothing odd that we're aware of," I said.

"Did anyone feel something strange move through them just before the spell started?" Rhett asked.

"Not me," Granny Dottie said, keeping a beady eye on Randal. "It all happened so quickly, though. One second, I was holding your hand, and the next, I was flying through the air and hit the wall. The kittens came with me. They pinned themselves to my chest like fluffy brooches."

"What's your ability? Could your magic have misfired?" Randal asked Rhett.

"Fallen angel. But not the kind you're thinking of. I'm a reformed magic user," he said. "My magic isn't all that. There's no way it did this."

"It's incredible what the love of a good Crypt witch will do to a man," I said. "But that's enough about our problems. Randal, you have your own trials. No one here is badly hurt, and you need help."

"If you need to go with your friend, then do so. I can look after things here," Granny Dottie said.

"What about finding Tempest?" Rhett said. "This won't wait."

"What about my friend?" Randal asked. "Erick is dead. What happened to him wasn't natural. He was the same age as me and healthy. Someone did this to him."

"There's enough of us to handle these problems," I said. "Dottie, Rhett, Vorana, and Sage, you focus on finding Tempest. Use location spells but be careful. We don't need a repeat of this."

Vorana looked around the smoky room and sighed. "I was thinking about redecorating. At least I have a good reason to do so."

"We'll go with Randal and figure out what happened," I said.

For a second, Zandra looked conflicted. She must want to find Tempest, but Randal was a good friend and clearly in distress. "Let's do it. If there's someone in town terrifying people to death, we have to stop them."

"We'll be as quick as we can," I said to Granny Dottie. "If you run into any roadblocks, we're easy to reach."

"You go. I'll make things right here," she said.

To save time, I cast a translocation spell to the address Randal told me. I was surprised to learn where he lived. His house came with a name, which suggested it wasn't cheap to buy. Perhaps he was just renting a room.

I was even more surprised when we arrived outside a huge three-story detached building in a mock Georgian design. It had sash windows, which were all open, and a double front door at the entrance, with impressive chimney stacks on either side of the building.

"This is where you live?" I asked him.

He shrugged, looking a touch embarrassed.

"With family members?"

"No, this is mine."

"Wait! You own this whole place?" Zandra asked. "How?"

"My freelance work outside of animal control pays well. And I co-produced a few apps and games that bring in regular dividends." Randal's cheeks glowed. "It's nothing."

"You live here on your own?" I was still peering at the enormous chimneys.

"Yeah, although I often have friends stay when we're working on a project," Randal said. He took a step toward the front door but then stopped. "I... I don't want to go inside."

"Stay out here for now," I said. "Let's start around the back. I'd like to check on Charlie and see if there's anything we can do to help him."

"I don't have strong healing magic, but I tried everything I could to get him to open his eyes," Randal said. "He was breathing, and I couldn't see any injuries, so I covered him with a blanket and left him. I needed to get help for Erick as fast as possible."

"We understand. It's natural to panic in a situation like this. I'll lead the way," I said.

Randal was clearly reluctant to look at his friend's body again, and I understood why. He hadn't stopped shaking since he'd arrived at Vorana's house and trudged behind us as if he carried an enormous weight on his back.

Zandra cast a light ball overhead, even though we had the benefit of the full moon to guide us. Randal's house had a vast backyard with an expansive lawn, a large porch with a table, a hammock, and a rocking chair. It was easy to spot where Charlie was, since Randal had covered him in a pale blanket.

"I'll look at Erick," Zandra said. "You see how Charlie is doing."

We headed off in opposite directions, Randal not keen to go with either of us, so he lingered on the edge of the lawn.

I dashed onto the porch and looked down at Charlie. He appeared to be asleep, his chest rising and falling in a regular rhythm. His eyes were closed and his expression relaxed. But as I got closer, there was a stink of old magic all over him. It turned my stomach and made my booping snooter twitch as if I'd just inhaled pungent pepper.

There was something grossly familiar about that smell, but I couldn't place it. Whoever had thrown this magic over Charlie must be as old as me. But it wasn't goddess power. It was something more primitive. And something I wanted to be nowhere near.

I spent a few moments inspecting Charlie, and once I was satisfied he was in no danger, I headed over to Erick.

Zandra was crouched beside his body, her brow furrowed.

She looked up as I approached. "He's gone. There's not a trace of life. He must have been dead for hours when Randal found him."

Randal inched closer, his arms wrapped around his middle, giving himself a hug. "I should have set the alarm when we came in, but nothing bad ever happens in this part of town. I was distracted because we were talking about the bar fight. That fight really spooked them."

"That fight wasn't your fault," I said.

"Sure. But I wasn't thinking straight when we got home. If the alarm had been set, I'd have heard someone come in and open the doors and windows. Why do that?"

"They could have used an element spell," Zandra said. "Elemental magic hates being trapped inside. Someone could have cast a spell to knock out you and Charlie and then attacked Erick."

"But we would have heard them," Randal said.

"What's the last thing you remember?" I asked.

Randal tore his eyes away from Erick's body. "I remember feeling tired. The guys said they wanted snacks, so I told them to help themselves. I just closed my eyes for what I thought were a few minutes, and that was it."

"Someone could have cast magic, but it affected you differently," I said. "You passed out, but Charlie and Erick were in a different room, so it didn't have such an effect on them. Maybe they came back in and found whoever it was. They made a run for it but were chased. Charlie was attacked on the porch and left for dead. Erick got farther, but for whatever reason, his attacker couldn't let him live."

"What about the fight at the bar?" Zandra asked. "Could someone have followed you back?"

"Why would they do that?" Randal asked.

"Revenge? Maybe you upset someone when you used your tech on them."

"Our tech didn't work. That's why Erick and Charlie were here. We planned on finding the gadgets' glitches and fixing them."

"Perhaps Erick's injuries were more serious than we realized," I said. "Did he complain of feeling unwell when he got back here?"

Randal shook his head. "I used a couple of pre-made healing spells on him to be on the safe side, but he felt fine. Although his nose wouldn't stop dripping, but that's nothing new."

"This attack messed with all of you," I said. "Charlie is out cold, and you don't remember what happened. I don't think you fell asleep. You were impacted by whoever did this."

"It could have been a spell gone wrong," Zandra said. "Whoever cast the spell needed you all unconscious, but they used too much magic on Erick, and it killed him."

"Why would they want us unconscious?" Randal asked.

"To steal from you," I said. "Have you noticed anything missing? Do you store valuables here?"

"I'm not into antiques, if that's what you mean," Randal said. "And I haven't looked around. I've been too stressed."

"What about your freelance work?" I asked. "You said it pays well."

"It does. I bought this house outright," Randal said with another embarrassed shrug.

"Are you working on anything at the moment?"

"We always have projects on the go with half-finished designs and apps."

"Anything particularly valuable?" Zandra asked. "Something worth killing over?"

Randal rubbed the back of his neck. "It's all got potential. I don't know, though. It's specialist stuff."

"Let's take a look around and see if anything is missing." I looked at Zandra. "And you need to call in Angel Force. Cythera must see this."

Zandra grimaced. "I get the worst jobs."

"You could stand guard over the body."

She sighed. "I'll call the angels."

Chapter 5

Question time

The clock in Randal's kitchen had just slid past four in the morning when two angels arrived on the scene. I did a double take when they walked in then bounced on my toe beans and raced over. Finn was back!

He grinned at me as I curled around his legs, my tail up. "Hey, Juno. It's good to see you, too."

"We thought you were never coming back to Crimson Cove," I said. "We assumed Bell had seduced you into staying with her for good."

"Crimson Cove will always have a place in my heart," Finn said. "But Bell's stolen a good chunk of it, too. We're figuring things out."

"How is Bell? And what about her companion, Hodgepodge? He was grumpily intriguing when we met."

"The dragons are keeping them busy," Finn said. "I was getting in the way, and—"

"And you have a job to do here," Cythera snapped, her expression icy. "Let's focus on that, shall we? Your love life is hardly an appropriate topic of conversation, given we're at a crime scene."

"Sorry, boss." Finn was still grinning. "It's good to see you, Zandra. Randal."

"You too. Although I wish it was under happier circumstances," Zandra said. "We've got a weird situation going on."

Cythera fluttered her wings. "And why are you both in the middle of this weirdness? It's Randal's friend who's dead, isn't it?"

Randal lifted a hand, as if waiting for permission to speak. "That's my fault. I asked Juno and Zandra for help. When I woke to chaos—Erick dead on the lawn and Charlie out cold, and I couldn't wake him—I knew I should have come to Angel Force, but I wasn't thinking."

Finn strode over and patted Randal's shoulder. "No worries. Of course, you'd panic when you find a body on the grass. I'm sorry you lost your friend."

"Thanks. It sucks. We've been trying to figure it out, but it's a mystery."

"Leave the figuring out to the experts," Cythera said. "You should have contacted us first. Having amateurs on the scene contaminates evidence."

"By now, you know we're far from amateurs," I said. "Nothing's been moved or unnecessarily touched. Although we have been looking around the house to see if whoever did this stole something of value. That could be a motive for this murder."

Cythera scowled at me. "You've tramped around everywhere? That's unhelpful."

"Did you find anything missing?" Finn asked.

"It was hard to determine," I said. "Randal isn't tidy. Although we already knew that from the state of his desk at animal control."

"I do my best," Randal said. "But I get distracted by new ideas. I forget about the ones I'm working on, so they sit there, waiting for my attention."

"You're good," Finn said. "But we're here now. And we have a few questions, if you're up to it."

"You need to be up to it," Cythera said. "This death happened on your property. What about your other friend? Where is he?"

"Charlie is unharmed, other than being unable to wake," I said. "I checked myself. He's in no distress."

"He should be in the hospital!"

"I wasn't sure if I should move him," Randal said. "There could be evidence you need to collect."

"Injuries come before evidence," Cythera said. "Let's look at him first, then we'll deal with everything else."

A few minutes later, Cythera was slightly less grumpy, and we'd arranged to have Charlie taken to the hospital to see if the doctors could wake him.

Randal watched him go, a forlorn look on his face. "Maybe when Charlie wakes, he'll be able to tell us what happened."

"Why don't you tell us what you know?" Finn guided Randal back to the house and into the kitchen. "Cythera will look around Erick's body and see if anything is amiss. You won't need to help with that, though."

Randal puffed out a sigh. "I feel useless. I couldn't protect my friends in my own home."

"You shouldn't need to protect them," I said, following a short distance behind Finn with Zandra. "You weren't to know this would happen. And this is the fancy part of town. It's safe."

"Juno's right. We rarely get called out this way," Finn said. "You've got a nice place."

"Thanks. If I had better magic, I'd have sensed something was wrong." Randal leaned against the marble kitchen counter. "I'm nothing without my gadgets."

"You're far from nothing." I hopped up beside Randal and leaned my head on his arm.

"Let's get the basic details and work our way from there," Finn said. "What were you doing this evening?"

Randal quickly recounted our evening together. He told Finn about the bar fight, and then coming back to the house with his friends.

"I heard about that fight," Finn said as he made notes. "Someone called it in. We're sending angels over in the morning to find out if any troublemakers rolled into town."

"We're stumped as to why the fight started," I said.

"Just as I am over what happened here," Randal said. "I sensed no trouble. It was an average evening."

"What about you two?" Finn looked at Zandra and me. "Did you notice anything strange going on with Randal's friends?"

"Both were obsessed with tech magic like Randal," I said. "Much of the talk went over my head. They love their gadgets."

"Same here," Zandra said. "They were showing off this new design they were working on."

"What does it do?" Finn asked Randal.

"It shrinks things," Randal said. "At least it's supposed to. It's been malfunctioning, though. We're also working on a couple of apps we want to sell to non-magicals. One is a streamlined ordering service. We've been seeing comments about how there is too much choice, and people can never decide what they want because there are a hundred different types of toothpaste and thirty different types of chocolate spread. Our app minimizes overwhelm. It's simple, but we've already sold the concept."

"Could a rival company be envious of your success?" I asked. "Maybe they wanted to steal the shrink gadget or your app and claim it was theirs?"

"There's always competition in this industry," Randal said. "But to kill someone over it? I can't see that happening."

"How much money are we talking?" Finn asked.

"A few million as the initial investment," Randal said. "Don't look surprised. It's not uncommon in tech development, especially in the non-magical community. There are so many of them, billions using apps. They want a simple life, and we're making apps that solve their problems. Everyone wins."

"That amount of money would make a lot of people do a lot of nasty things to get their hands on it," I said.

"They wouldn't get their hands on any money if they took the tech or the app idea," Randal said.

"The investors already have our prototype designs, so anyone coming out with an identical product would be revealed as a fraud."

"And the shrink machine?" Finn asked.

"I suppose it could be used by criminals," Randal said. "But they wouldn't want to touch it with what it's doing at the moment. We've yet to figure out the glitch. It sometimes miniaturizes things, but it also super-sizes them."

"If the glitches were worked out, it could have multiple applications?" I asked.

"Sure. But I've invented stuff similar to this before," Randal said. "No one's broken into my house, opened the doors and windows, and tried to kill me and my friends. This is nothing special. And it won't be the first on the market. We were just making refinements."

"Do you have any enemies?" Finn asked. "Or your friends? Someone who wanted you out of the picture?"

Randal appeared stunned as he scrubbed at his chin. "I keep my head down and my mouth shut most of the time. I'm either busy in animal control, dealing with the wards and system glitches, or out on assignments in other parts of the country. Other than a few close friends and people I work with, I don't see anyone to make an enemy of."

"Randal is charming," I said. "I only imagine people liking him."

"You've got serious assets," Finn said. "Maybe someone's jealous of your success."

"I can't think of anyone in town who'd be like that," Randal said. "At least no one comes to mind."

Finn glanced around the kitchen as he scratched his head. "Maybe we'll find evidence when we look around. Keep thinking. I'll go and check on Cythera, see if she's found anything. And don't worry about Erick's body. Once we've gotten everything we need, we'll be careful when moving him. We'll need to run tests to see what actually killed him. There'll be an autopsy."

Randal closed his eyes for several seconds and swallowed loudly. "I should tell his family. I don't know how I'll break the news to them."

"We can do that," Finn said. "It's all part of the job."

"No, I'll do it. Thanks for the offer, though."

Finn patted Randal on the shoulder then nodded at us before heading out to join Cythera.

"You look exhausted," Zandra said to Randal. "Will you be able to sleep?"

"Not here!" He looked around with alarm in his eyes. "I have a camp bed at work. Sometimes, when I stay late, I crash there."

"That can't be comfortable," Zandra said.

"I like it. I can hear the animals out back in the pens. I sometimes hang out with them. I'll go there. I know it's secure. I'll be too jumpy if I stay in my own bed tonight."

Zandra walked over and hugged him. "I'm sorry this happened. We'll get justice for your friends. And for you."

After a second of freezing in place, Randal hugged her back. "Thanks. That means a lot. I knew I could rely on you for help."

"We always help a friend in need," I said. "Walk out with us. We'll let the angels know where we're going."

After updating Cythera, we left the crime scene and walked in silence through the eerily quiet streets. Crimson Cove was still. Not another person around at such a late hour.

We stopped when we reached animal control and waited for Randal to unlock the door and turn off the alarm.

"We could stay," I said.

"But we'd be more productive chasing up this crime," Zandra said.

"I'm good here. This place feels like my second home. If I can't sleep, we've got a couple of golden-eared pheasants in the pens. I love their light shows."

"We'll give you an update as soon as we have one," I said.

We said our goodbyes and waited until the door had closed and the locks were slid back into place before leaving.

"We're not going home, are we?" Zandra asked.

"The bar fight is playing on my mind," I said. "Something odd went down there. I don't want to wait for the angels to investigate in the morning. The evidence could have vanished by then."

"Then let's go back to the bar," Zandra said. "I'm too hyped up to sleep, anyway."

We decided to walk, since we needed to clear our heads. This was a puzzling mystery. Randal was the most decent and honest person I knew. He had no airs and graces and never bragged about just how ridiculously wealthy he was. The man spent his life in sneakers, badly fitting jeans, and T-shirts. He ate basic food and slept at work. It was unlikely anyone knew how much money he had, so they wouldn't have come after him for his wealth.

"We must make sure the angels look into Charlie and Erick's backgrounds," I said. "Perhaps the attacker is linked to them, not Randal. They could have followed them to Crimson Cove and sprung their attack."

"Why attack now, though?" Zandra asked. "It would have been easier to get them on their own."

"Perhaps. Maybe Erick or Charlie did something to enrage their attacker, and they lost control. And since Erick is dead, we'll focus on him."

"Now Finn is here, it'll be easier to get information from Angel Force," Zandra said. "It's good to have him home. Bertoli was decent enough. Cythera, not so much. But Finn is easy going."

"Where is Bertoli?" I asked. "I haven't seen him recently."

"I heard from Barney that he's taken time off after the ordeal with his Academy friends."

"Poor Bertoli. That angel lives on his nerves," I said. "After everything that happened to him, he deserves a break. We'll send him a gift basket. Do you know where he went?"

"No. And I doubt he wants to be reminded of us," Zandra said. "Let's leave the gift for now. Any reminders from Crimson Cove might stir bad memories."

"He'll be happy to get a gift from us. We're excellent friends these days. Even closer since we spent Christmas together. Bertoli really is an excellent cook."

"We uncovered the fact he didn't have any friends at his training academy," Zandra said. "Bertoli was badly bullied, and everyone thought he was weird. Do you think he wants that truth revealed or nudged back to the top of his thoughts?"

"As if we'd gossip about such a thing. Besides, weirdness is wonderful. It makes a person unique. This world has gotten too used to its cookie-cutter characters and airbrushed perfection. I was nosing around some of these sites Randal is obsessed with, and everyone looks the same. The same hair and face. Where's all the difference? The lumps and bumps and quirks that make everything delightful? You wipe out the difference, and you have nothing special. Boredom. And when people are bored, they misbehave. And we know where bad behavior leads."

"I stay away from all that," Zandra said. "It makes me miserable."

"Why bother looking at the make-believe when real life is far more fascinating?" I asked.

We reached the bar a few minutes later. The broken window was boarded over, and the debris outside had been cleared away.

We tested the doors, but none were accessible. The same with the windows. It was an easy enough magic trick to bypass the security locks and get inside.

"Woah! You'd never know there'd been a fight here." Zandra stood with her hands on her hips, surveying the scene. Anything broken had vanished and damaged furniture replaced with new.

"This won't have been the first bar fight this place has experienced," I said. "There must be spares of everything out the back."

We spent a few minutes walking around but found nothing to reveal why the fight started or if it was connected to what happened to Randal and his friends.

I drew in a deep breath, and my booping snooter wrinkled. It was faint, but there was a weird vibe about this place.

I yelped and rolled over several times as something sharp and painful landed on my back. A second later, it was joined by something equally unpleasant. My magic activated and swirled around me as I prepared to retaliate.

"Stop! It's the kittens! Don't blast them." Zandra was racing toward me from the other side of the bar.

I pulled back the spell I'd intended to shoot out and hissed fiercely. The third kitten made his appearance, fluffed up like a tiny black marshmallow, his brilliant green eyes sparkling with magical mischief.

I yanked one of the kittens off my belly just before she bit me. "You're supposed to be at home. Granny Dottie is looking after you."

The kittens danced around, attempting to engage me in a fight.

I boxed one of them about the ears. "Enough of that. This is serious business, and you're interfering."

"They must be missing you," Zandra said.

"They should be asleep. It's well past their bedtime."

"Ours too." Zandra tugged on the end of her hair. "There's nothing useful here. All the evidence will have been swept away."

"Why clear the bar so quickly? It doesn't open early, so they could have done it tomorrow." I grabbed one of the kittens as he attempted to dart away. "Maybe Angel Force will uncover something when they question the employees."

Zandra frowned at nothing in particular. "Let's go home. I want to see if there's been progress with finding Tempest."

"Of course. We need to get back to your family," I said. "Help me with these fluffy nightmares."

Zandra grabbed two of the squirming, protesting kittens, while I tossed the third onto my back. We headed to the door and stepped out into the night.

Zandra glanced up at the moon. "A missing sister and a dead body. What next? A rabid yeti chasing us along the street?"

I chuckled. "Well, they say it always comes in threes."

Chapter 6

Storm brewing

"Was Erick a decent guy?" Vorana served freshly made pancakes to Zandra and herself, after having set the kitchen table and given me and Sage our usual morning plates of salmon and scrambled eggs. "He came by the bookstore yesterday and seemed nice enough, although he did flirt with me in a kind of creepy way. He browsed with his friend and Randal for over an hour, and they left with full bags of books."

"No offense to the dead, but Erick was a lousy flirter," Zandra said. "He wouldn't take the hint that I wasn't interested."

"It's a mystery what happened," I said after swallowing a large mouthful of delicious salmon. "Erick dead on the grass and Charlie in a magically induced coma."

"And Randal slept through the whole thing," Zandra said.

"Erick and Charlie must have tried to escape," I said. "Randal said they went to the kitchen to get food. Whoever was after them blasted out a spell, intending for them to fall asleep, but it didn't reach far enough into the house to affect Charlie and Erick. They must have come back to the living room, seen their attacker, and legged it."

"Would they have abandoned Randal if someone was throwing out dangerous magic?" Vorana sipped her coffee.

"They're tech mages, not warriors," Zandra said. "If they weren't armed with one of their weird gadgets, they'd have been powerless."

"As we witnessed during the bar fight, tech mages can only summon basic magic when they have no gadgets to act as conduits," I said. "Whoever went after them must have known they'd be easy to stop."

"They could have run to get a gadget, got cut off, and then escaped out the back to go get help," Zandra said.

"And whoever it was couldn't let them get away because they'd be able to tell Angel Force who their attacker was." Vorana's mug had stopped halfway to her mouth, she was so engrossed in the conversation. "You still don't know why this mysterious attacker went to Randal's house? Was it a planned break-in? Was someone after Randal and his friends, or did they just get unlucky?"

"We looked around with Randal to see if anything had been taken," I said, "but he's not the tidiest person, so it was hard to know for sure."

"Some of the rooms looked like they'd been turned over, but Randal said that's how they always look. The guy is messy," Zandra said.

"You can be a slouch in the cleaning department too," I said.

"I keep the basement clean. I have to, or I'd be tripping over stuff all the time," Zandra said.

"You're always losing your keys."

"But I always find them again." She grinned at me.

"Hopefully, Randal will have gotten some sleep and will be clearheaded this morning," I said. "We could take him back to his house and do another walk-through. He might spot if anything was taken more easily in the daylight."

"And when he's less shocked. What about his friend, Charlie?" Vorana asked. "Any news on him?"

"The angels arranged for him to go to the hospital," I said. "When I sniffed around him, I smelled strange magic. Something primitive. I couldn't put my paw on it, but it was old magic."

"You'd know about old magic," Sage muttered out of the side of her mouth.

"You focus on your salmon," I muttered back. "We're looking for an experienced magic user. Someone who's not scared of ancient spells. Certainly not someone who'd enjoy tech magic. It probably makes their skin crawl."

"Why would someone using ancient spells be interested in tech mage magic?" Zandra asked. "The two don't mix."

Vorana nodded. "It reminds me of the arguments when e-books first came on the scene. So many people were up in arms because they thought it was the death of the paperback. For a time, I was worried about my store. But people still love their paperbacks and the special editions. There's a place for both. The same goes for magic."

"Some of the old-school magic users don't agree when it comes to tech magic," I said. "They think it's unnatural to combine spells with technology."

"They're scared it'll be the rise of the robots." Vorana chuckled as she fired imaginary laser blasts from her fingertips. "They'll take over and eliminate us."

"Magically infused robots. There's a thought," I said. "It could have its place."

"Were Randal and his friends working on anything in particular?" Vorana asked. "Something that would unsettle other magic users?"

"Randal talked about a couple of projects but nothing alarming," I said. "An app and shrink tech."

The whole time we'd been talking, Zandra kept checking her mobile snow globe, which she had perched on her knee. She'd been doing it throughout the night, too. There was still no news about Tempest.

I finished my breakfast, squeezed onto her lap, and leaned against her chest. "As soon as there's anything new, you'll be the first to hear."

When we'd returned last night, Vorana gave us an update on the unsuccessful attempts to locate Tempest. She'd tried for over an hour with Granny Dottie and Rhett, but the location spells refused to work. They kept fizzling out or sparking, trying to set fire to things. And since one of Vorana's rooms was currently still smoke charred and too dangerous to go into because of the last fire, they'd called it quits.

Granny Dottie and Rhett had returned to Willow Tree Falls to continue a local search, and Vorana had fallen into bed after exhausting her magic.

Even though Zandra hadn't complained or fretted, she was worried about her missing sister.

Tempest Crypt was one of the most powerful witches I'd ever met. She could spot a demon's weakness, hunt them out, and bend them to her will. Her name was legendary among the demon community. They despised her.

Whatever it was and whatever means and methods needed, we'd find Tempest. I had to ensure my wonderful witch was happy again. And she wouldn't be happy until Tempest was back, whipping demon behind and chasing after Wiggles while he misbehaved.

A knock at the front door sent Vorana out to answer it. She returned a few seconds later with her boyfriend, Brodie, a surly warrior angel. He had Randal with him. Neither of them looked happy. Randal's hair stood on end, suggesting he'd been running his fingers through it repeatedly. He was still in last night's clothes. Brodie looked like he'd just stepped off the battlefield. He was bruised, and there was blood on his clothing and smeared through his feathers.

"Both of you, sit," Vorana said. "Brodie, let me give you something for those bruises. And if you want to wash up before we talk, go right ahead."

He briefly kissed her cheek. "In a few minutes, babe. This is official business."

"At least sit and have a coffee," Vorana said. "You both look exhausted."

"How did you sleep?" I asked Randal, keeping an eye on the battle soiled angel. What manner of power had messed with him so effectively?

"I couldn't sleep. I kept thinking about what happened." There were dark smudges under Randal's eyes. "Every time I closed my eyes, I kept seeing Erick. And I've just been to visit Charlie. He's the same. The doctors can't figure out what's wrong with him. They know it's magic keeping him under, but the spell is muddled. Such a mess."

"And it's about to get messier," Brodie said. "We found evidence at the scene. There was something written in the dirt."

"A clue as to who attacked Erick?" I asked.

"I saw nothing last night," Zandra said. "I checked carefully."

"We only noticed it when we moved Erick's body," Brodie said. "He must have propped himself onto his side, dug his finger in the dirt, and then fallen on it."

Zandra nodded, her eyes narrowing a fraction. "What was it?"

Randal shifted beside Brodie, while Brodie stood upright and placed his hands behind his back.

"The suspense is too much," I said. "What was written in the dirt?"

"Erick wrote the word Tempest." Brodie looked at Zandra, a muscle ticking in his stubbled jaw.

Zandra stared back, unblinking. "And you think he meant my sister?"

"She's been in Crimson Cove recently. And we all know she's a troubled witch. Does she have—"

"Tempest isn't troubled." Zandra shoved back her chair, scooping me onto her shoulder. "Tempest helps Angel Force. She's always helped you, though you never appreciate it. This murder has nothing to do with her. Remove that sneaky thought from your head."

"We don't have any Tempests living in Crimson Cove," Randal said.

"So, you instantly assume it was my sister?" Zandra's hand was shaking as she held me close.

"Does Tempest know Erick?" Brodie asked.

"No! At least, I don't think so," Zandra said. "Tempest isn't into tech magic. She has no problem with it, but it's not something any of us are big on. Tech magic and demons don't merge well. We stick with the old stuff."

"Then why would Erick write her name in the dirt?" There was a whisper of a quiver in Randal's voice.

"It wasn't Tempest! Why do you keep saying it was her?" Zandra snapped.

"I... I, well, we don't know another Tempest," Randal said. "I've racked my brain, and we have no contacts with that name. It's also an unusual name for a witch."

"Maybe it's a surname, not a first name," I said. "Has Angel Force checked for any criminals with that last name? Anyone called Tempest who has a problem with Erick?"

"Yes! Do that, instead of jabbing a finger at my family," Zandra said.

"We have. We've been working through the night," Brodie said on a sigh. "Don't automatically think we saw that name and thought of your sister. We kept it quiet because we needed to do some checks. Randal went through his old contacts to see if there was a connection but came up blank. We did the same with our records. We got nothing."

Zandra huffed out a breath. "So, you came back to my family? Thanks for nothing." She was glaring at Randal.

He pressed his lips together. "What am I supposed to do? My friend was murdered! And your sister was in town recently. She does have a temper."

"Erick wasn't here, then! They've never met. Even if they had, Erick wouldn't have annoyed Tempest enough to do this. It's not her style."

"What is her style?" Brodie's tone was icy.

"If it's not a demon, then she's not bothered," Zandra said. "That's Tempest's specialty. She has the skills to make your lives easier. She takes problem demons off the streets. That's her obsession. Not troubling nerdy tech mages who prefer looking at screens to interacting with people."

"Our tech helps people!" Randal said. "People get pleasure from our games and apps as well. You make it sound like what I do is worthless."

"And Brodie is making it sound as if what my sister does makes her unstable and likely to lash out at people she doesn't know for no reason," Zandra said. "Show me the logic in that assumption."

"That's not what I meant." Brodie gestured for Zandra to lower her tone. "But we need to speak to Tempest. Where is she?"

Zandra drew in a shaky breath. "You can't speak to her."

"If we're to eliminate her from our inquiries, we at least need a conversation. Make sure she has an alibi and no motive for wanting Erick dead," Brodie said.

"You're talking like you think she's guilty," Zandra said.

I sent a wave of calming magic over Zandra, since her power fizzled beneath her skin as she struggled to hold in her rage.

"Brodie, where exactly did you get those injuries?" Vorana asked quietly.

He rubbed his forehead. "When we found Tempest's name—"

"A word!" Zandra said. "You found a word in the dirt, written by a terrified, dying man. It doesn't mean it was her name. Get your facts in order."

"My witch is right," I said. "Tempest could also mean a storm. Trouble brewing. It doesn't automatically point to this being the work of a Crypt witch."

"Fine. When we found this particular word in the dirt, we visited Willow Tree Falls to speak to Tempest," Brodie growled out.

"And you found her?" I cocked my head as a worrying thought trickled through me. How did Brodie get those injuries? He was a trained fighter and knew how to handle himself. Whoever had roughed him up must have been powerful. Were they Crypt witch powerful?

"We tracked Tempest to the woods in the village. She was hanging out close to an old stone circle up the hill. The second we found her, things went wrong."

"Wrong how? Wait a second. Are you saying Tempest did this to you?" Zandra asked.

"Tempest and her small hound," Brodie said. "Tempest went first, and the hound backed her up. Then they vanished."

Zandra opened her mouth then snapped it shut. "I don't believe you. You're mistaken. Are you sure you had the right person? Did you attack first? Tempest and Wiggles wouldn't attack someone without good reason."

"Everyone in Angel Force knows your sister," Brodie said. "Tempest has a reputation."

"For helping to save your butts more times than you care to remember. I'm not happy with this. I need to speak to Cythera." Zandra flicked her wrist, casting a translocation spell and taking me with her.

We appeared outside Angel Force in a flash of her spiky magic, revealing just how prickled her temper was

"Take a moment to calm yourself before you charge inside," I said. "I know it's a shock that Angel Force considers Tempest a suspect, but going in all magic blazing will make this worse."

"How can this get any worse? Brodie has to be lying. I've never liked that guy. He's always off, supposedly working, and leaving Vorana alone. What's he really doing? Being shady, that's what." Zandra was already stomping toward the building. "Tempest has no reason to attack anyone. Not Randal or Brodie. And she had no reason to kill Erick."

"We'll get to the bottom of this. Someone has made a massive mistake."

"And I'll make them pay for it." Zandra stormed into the open-plan office.

Finn appeared out of the kitchen, a mug of coffee in his hand. His expression shifted the second he saw how furious Zandra was, and he hurried over.

"You've heard the news?" he asked.

"What's going on?" Zandra said. "Which feather-brained pencil pusher thinks Tempest has anything to do with this murder?"

Finn rested a hand on her shoulder. "We're just following the evidence."

"Just making massive assumptions." Zandra shrugged his hand away. "Do you really think my sister is guilty because of a word a dying man scrawled in the dirt?"

Cythera strode out of her office, her wings fluttering. "How did you find out?"

"Your knuckle-headed former warrior angel has been making wrongful accusations," Zandra said.

"Brodie could have been more tactful when asking about Tempest," I said.

"He thinks she's unstable, and he accused Tempest and Wiggles of attacking him! Why would they do that?" Zandra asked.

I'd defend my witch to the end of time, but I couldn't forget how worried Wiggles was when Tempest went missing. And Granny Dottie and Rhett wouldn't have shown up if there wasn't a problem.

I kept quiet, not wanting to add fuel to Angel Force's belief Tempest had anything to do with this murder. She wasn't involved.

"We have good reason to think it was Tempest behind this attack," Cythera said. "And not just because of what Erick wrote before he died. We've had numerous reports of her eccentric behavior."

"No doubt from your angel friends in Willow Tree Falls," Zandra spat. "They've never liked her despite all the help she's given them over the years. The demons she's gotten off the streets. The lives she's saved because the demons are gone. Tempest has never been appreciated. I don't know why she bothers with you."

"Because she's a good witch," I said. "Zandra is correct. Tempest only ever has an issue with demons."

"She must have made a mistake." Cythera lifted her chin and stared down at Zandra. "Crypt witch magic is ancient. Old magic mutates into something deadly if used incorrectly."

"You're accusing Tempest of being unable to control her powers?" Zandra shook her head, her hands flexing repeatedly. "She's saved the day so many times I've lost count. Now, one tiny situation appears, and you've forgotten all of that."

"Calm yourself. No one has been charged with anything," Cythera said.

"We're simply gathering information," Finn said. "It's still early in the investigation."

Cythera rolled her shoulders. "We know you're close and you've been in contact recently. You'll be helping us by revealing her location. All we want to do is have a civilized conversation with her."

"What you want to do is tear apart Tempest's alibi and accuse her of a crime she hasn't committed. You'll get nothing from me." Magic flared on Zandra's fingers.

Before she could cast the spell she was summoning, I whisked us away, and we landed in the middle of Crimson Cove Woods, far from Angel Force and anyone who might cause us trouble.

Zandra thrust out the spell she'd meant to blast the angels with, and it ricocheted around the trees before slowly fading to nothing. "Those dumb angels! Tempest always thought they were stupid, and this proves how right she was."

"We'll prove them wrong," I said. "They've made mistakes before."

"Nothing like this! What are they thinking? They aren't thinking. They're scared and jumping on nothing clues."

I sent another wave of calming magic over Zandra. "We'll fix it."

"We will," Zandra said after doing some deep breathing. "We'll find Erick's killer and demand a very public, very large, and very humiliating apology from Angel Fools. They'll be sorry they ever accused Tempest of murder. And we're starting now!"

Chapter 7

Tricky talk

"Before we interrogate and obliterate, you need a time out." I was perched on Zandra's shoulder as she paced back and forth among the trees, muttering to herself, sparks of magic sizzling off her fingertips. "If you speak to anyone in this mood, you'll get nowhere. They'll be so scared of you, they'll run off as fast as they can."

"I'm not waiting around doing nothing!" she said. "Finn will help us."

"Finn's busy. And Cythera will be watching you like a hawk. If you charge back into Angel Force, you'll lock talons and shred each other to pieces. You almost blasted her with a spell!"

Zandra shook out her hands and grimaced. "I got angry. Cythera wasn't listening. She never does. I won't let them go after Tempest."

"We'll stop them, and we'll find out what happened to Erick and Charlie. But crashing around like a marauding honey badger with a hangover will create roadblocks and trouble. I know this is personal, and you want to make sure

Tempest comes to no harm, but we need to keep clear heads and tackle this logically."

"Would you be tackling this logically if a member of your family was under suspicion of murder?"

"Perhaps not, but I would listen to my most trusted companion and take a time out when it was suggested," I said. "I'll start the groundwork. Go and get a strong coffee and the sweetest muffin Sorcha has on offer. Twenty minutes of sitting in the café and ruminating over a hot drink will help."

"It's a waste of time. The sooner we find Tempest, the sooner we can get her to safety and prove to the angels they were wrong about her," Zandra said.

"Vorana, Sage, Granny Dottie, and Rhett tried to find her last night. For whatever reason, Tempest doesn't want to be found," I said.

"Because she has Angel Force charging after her. Brodie must have done something to make her think he'd hurt her. She'd never strike without good reason." Zandra paced some more, her boots crunching over leaves and snapping dry twigs.

"There'll be an explanation. But a hothead and sparking magic won't help us uncover it. Go to the café."

A sizzle of magic shot out of Zandra's hand and pinged against a tree. "Maybe I do need to calm down. My anger is literally spilling out of me. I've never felt like this before."

"Because Tempest has never found herself in such trouble with the angels," I said.

"She's skirted the line plenty of times," Zandra said. "And they've accused her of murder before. I thought they had an understanding. She's on their side. Why are they so quick to forget that when something like this happens?"

"Angels are old-fashioned and slow to change," I said. "They hate things being different. It wasn't so long ago that the Academy only let purebred angels in for training."

"And then they relaxed the rules, and it almost got the whole place blown apart by a sneaky demon." Zandra blew out a breath. "Not that I'm defending the angels. What they're doing is wrong. They wouldn't manage if we withdrew our support. What would happen if we opened the door to the demon prison in Willow Tree Falls? Would Angel Force be able to handle the chaos?"

"No, and they're aware of that," I said. "Angel Force is supposed to be the key peacekeeping and law enforcement body in most magical towns. It must rub them the wrong way to know they can't do their job properly without outside support."

Zandra scraped her hair off her face and kissed my side. "I'll go chill. But let me know as soon as you find something. What will you do?"

"I need a conversation with Randal, so it's best you're not there," I said.

Her eyes narrowed. "I never want to see him again. He must have snitched to Angel Force about Tempest."

"An angel found the word beneath Erick's body," I said. "Randal had nothing to do with it."

"Randal is glad Tempest is in trouble. He's terrified of her. She grilled him for ages when she visited over the holidays."

"Tempest likes Randal. She told me. Now go. Get something hot and caffeinated and something sugary to stuff into your mouth. I'll meet you at animal control. We may need some time off to deal with this situation, so we'll have to fix things with Barney."

We went our separate ways. I returned to Vorana's, but Brodie and Randal had already left. Vorana directed me to Randal's house, so I magicked my way there and found Randal sitting out the front of the house by the door, his head resting in his hands.

He scrambled to his feet as soon as I appeared. "Where's Zandra?"

"Taking a suggested time out," I said. "We need to talk."

"I'm sorry I offended her," he said. "I'm so worried about Charlie not making it, and I can't get my head around what happened to Erick. I keep expecting him to walk outside and start talking about some new project. Of course, that won't happen now."

I gestured for him to sit back down and hopped onto the porch. "Have you had news about when the angels will finish their tests on Erick's body to confirm the cause of death?"

"They said it would be a day or two. Maybe that'll give us a clue about what happened."

"Let's hope so," I said. "Because one thing I'm sure of. Tempest Crypt had nothing to do with this."

Randal closed his eyes for a second. "Do you think Zandra will ever talk to me again?"

I thought back to their conversation. "Zandra is stubborn, so give her time. She's worried about

Tempest. Once we figure out what happened here, she'll ease up on you."

"Did I sound like I was accusing Tempest when we were at Vorana's?" Randal asked. "I didn't mean to, but that was where my mind jumped straightaway."

"You and Brodie seemed focused on Tempest as Erick's killer," I said. "Why would that be?"

"I wouldn't have been so suspicious, but when Brodie tracked Tempest and Wiggles back to Willow Tree Falls and tried to talk to her, why did she attack him?"

"That is a mystery," I said. "Is Brodie absolutely sure it was Tempest?"

"Yeah, he knew her," Randal said. "And she's got that unique sidekick. The little guy who smells funny. Wiggles?"

"He is unique," I said. "He was once a regular dog, changed by magic. There was an incident with a car. Tempest refused to let him go, and her sister helped her to bring him back. He came back... different. As I understand it, Tempest used demon magic to ensure Wiggles will live for as long as she does."

"That's the kind of magic I'd love to wield," Randal said. "It would be amazing if your pets lived as long as you. I've seen people heartbroken and grieving when they lose a familiar. Do you remember what Barney was like?"

"I wasn't around at that time," I said. "But he still felt the loss of his familiar sharply when we started working at animal control."

"Of course. You hadn't moved here then," Randal said. "It tore him up. I'm glad he's found Ember. They work well together."

"They do. And I agree that kind of magic would be sublime. Most magic is helpful. And even though Tempest has brushed against the wrong side of the law more than once, her magic is good, too. All the Crypt witches have a strong desire to ensure justice is done. Otherwise, they wouldn't endure dealing with their foul demon prison."

"Yeah, I guess. I don't know, though. My head is scrambled." Randal scrubbed at his eyes.

"Let's start at the beginning," I said. "Would you like to go inside where it's more comfortable?"

Randal glanced over his shoulder and shuddered. "I'm not ready to go back in. I might just sell the place. Although, who'd want to buy it after what happened here? I guess I could rent it out."

"Give yourself time," I said. "You could always have the yard cleansed. Magic will heal it. Make the place feel good again."

"I suppose. Does Zandra know how to do that? Cleanse a place?"

"She does. And so do I. We'll make things right. But first, we need to learn more about Erick. How did you meet?"

Randal settled back against the porch railings. "We were friends online for years. We'd chat in different rooms and play the same games. One evening, I talked about an idea I had, and he got so excited. I knew he had skills and was a tech mage, too. Erick was the one who suggested we meet in person for a coffee so we could talk through the project."

"You've known each other for years, then."

"Yes. It wasn't long after meeting that we worked on a joint project together. The guy was brimming with ideas."

"Have you ever disagreed about your work?" I asked.

"Not really. Nothing bad. Sometimes we don't agree on the magic to use in a particular bit of tech, but we'd test and experiment. That's what we loved doing."

"There were no hard feelings if your idea beat his?"

"Nope. We'd partner on stuff equally. If we developed an app or a bit of tech together, we'd share right down the middle. Sometimes I'd put in more effort than him, but then he'd do the same the next go around. It's an equal partnership. Well, it was."

"And what about Charlie?"

"Much the same. He's more into the app side of things, though. He wants to blend magic into the non-magical community to make their lives easier. I'm less interested in that. I see there's way more money to be made from doing it, but that's not where my passion lies. I love gadgets. I love to tinker. So did Erick."

"What about any business rivals?" I asked. "The way you talked last night, it sounded like there's money to be made from your tinkering. That must make some people jealous."

Randal shook his head. "I've been thinking about this ever since Finn asked me, but there's no one in our community who'd commit murder. We're not like that. We're explorers and adventurers. We cheer each other on and congratulate when someone has a success."

"Erick never argued with anybody?" I asked. "We can't get along happily with everyone. That would be impossible."

"If he met someone he didn't get on with, he'd move on. He'd say they weren't the right person for him, that they'd fit better somewhere else. He never held a grudge or had any bad feelings toward anyone."

"What about problems in his private life?" I asked. "Any issues with a partner?"

"Erick was like me in that area, too." A faint flush colored Randal's cheeks. "He saw women he liked, but he did nothing about it."

"He was keen on Zandra."

"Was he? I didn't notice."

I'd have arched an eyebrow if I had them. "You missed him trying to hold her hand? And he invited her back to your house after the bar fight. Erick was sweet on Zandra."

"Who wouldn't be?"

"Didn't that make you jealous?"

"I'm not with Zandra."

"But you like her?"

Randal paused. "I do. But sometimes, a guy needs to know when to throw in the towel."

"That's what you've done? You're no longer interested in my wonderful witch?"

87

Randal stared at the ground. "Let's move on."

I studied Randal, not believing anyone would give up on Zandra. "Erick didn't get lonely?"

"Erick was too busy to be lonely," Randal said. "We didn't meet in person often, but we'd always talk online. Several times a day. And we'd play games as well. If he wasn't doing his day job, he was working on a side project, often with me or Charlie."

"Where did Erick work?"

"At an alternative tech firm. They run out of Star Valley. It's where the advanced tech magic is located. It's a company called Dilbert Innovations. Dilbert Dimitri runs the place. It's one of the top tech companies to work for if you're looking to make a name for yourself."

"Erick was happy there?"

"He was. Although they didn't pay him enough. I told him that several times, but he said he made enough from his sideline projects. And he liked the routine. He'd get there at the same time every day, eat the same meals, work at the same desk, and speak to the same people. Erick enjoyed order. He didn't do well in chaos."

"The way you work must have infuriated him, then," I said.

Randal chuckled. "He mentioned my mess more than once, but when he realized I wouldn't change, anything that bothered him, he cleared up himself. That was fine by me."

"What about Erick's family? You said you were going to talk to them."

Randal sighed. "I haven't yet, but I will. He's got a sister, Jazzi, and a brother, Langdon. No parents alive. How should I do it? How do you break this kind of news?"

"Angel Force can tell them," I said. "Finn has already offered."

"I want to. It happened at my house. I feel partly responsible."

"Talk me through Erick's movements on the night he died. When did you last see him alive?" I asked. "You were in shock last night, so you could have missed something that'll help us unpick this mystery."

Randal hesitated. "I'm a suspect, aren't I?"

"I could lie and say I have no idea what you're talking about, but Erick was your friend, and he died in your backyard. If I didn't get all the relevant details from you, including your alibi, I wouldn't be doing a good job, would I?"

He scratched his chin. "I understand. But I promise, I didn't murder Erick."

"I don't doubt that, but just stick to the facts, Randal."

"Sure. The facts." He ran a hand through his hair.

"You said Erick and Charlie left you on your own last night after you got back from the bar?"

"That's right. I was tired and needed a break, and they got hungry. They went off together. I could hear them talking, but I must have dozed off. Maybe it was the magic. Whatever attacked us had force to it."

"Is there anything else you remember before you dozed off?" I asked. "Any odd sounds or smells? Anything out of the ordinary?"

"It's just as I said. They left the room, I closed my eyes, and the next thing, I opened them to a freezing room and found my friends outside. That's when I came to you for help."

I looked at the house. "I know you won't want to do this, but I need your eyes to see if anything has been taken. This could be as simple as a robbery gone wrong."

Randal sucked in several breaths then pushed himself up. "I'll do it. Angel Force said I can go back in. They've collected everything they need."

"Did they find anything useful?"

"No, but they're keeping things close to their chest," he said. "Probably because they're thinking the same as you."

I rested a paw on Randal's leg. "I don't think you're a killer. And neither do the angels."

Randal twisted his mouth to the side. "Because of the whole Tempest thing?"

"Because of the whole Tempest thing."

"Should I send Zandra flowers as a way to make it up to her?"

I led the way to the entrance, since Randal seemed reluctant to move, and pushed open the front door. "She's not a fan of flowers. If you want to send her anything, make it something sweet and edible. Nothing hard, just in case she throws it at you."

"I've made a mess of things between us, haven't I?" Randal reluctantly stepped into the hallway and ducked as if he expected something to attack.

"You were panicked and upset. Zandra will figure that out. Should we start in the living room?"

Randal nodded. "I call it the games room. It's where I have most of my stations. You know, games consoles."

We spent a few minutes looking around the room, but Randal found nothing out of the ordinary, and I sensed nothing unusual.

"I can't figure out why Erick did it," Randal said as he led me into the kitchen.

"You mean writing Tempest on the ground?" I asked.

"Yes! And why did Tempest attack Brodie? If her magic is malfunctioning, she may not realize what she's doing. Did she hunt Erick because she thought he was a demon? And when Brodie approached her, she could have hallucinated he was something bad. That could have happened, right?"

That same concerning thought had also occurred to me. "Jumping to conclusions helps no one. And don't mention this theory to Zandra, or she really will never speak to you again."

Randal looked around the kitchen, his face a mask of helplessness. "I just want to find out what happened to my friends."

"We will. I promise," I said. "Do you know what Angel Force has planned next?"

Randal's eye twitched. "Maybe."

"Will you share?"

He tapped the tips of his fingers on the countertop. "They've got an all-points bulletin out for Tempest and Wiggles. They're the prime suspects."

I twitched my booping snooter. It was time to get serious. I had to find Tempest and Wiggles or Erick's killer. I didn't mind what task I achieved first, but I wouldn't rest until I knew the Crypt witches were in the clear and my own witch could relax, knowing her family was safe.

Chapter 8

Recharge

Randal had illuminated more questions than answers, and while he had my sympathy, I needed someone who would act and find a solution, not present me with more puzzles to ponder.

Action required energy, so I stopped for snacks at Sorcha's café. It was also a great place to catch up on local gossip. Sorcha always had her finger on the pulse.

I studied the chalkboard menu behind the counter as Sorcha served a customer, although I already knew what I'd have.

Sorcha looked down at me and smiled as the customer left, her bright ginger curls poking out from underneath a jaunty headscarf. "I'm glad you stopped by. I need your help."

"Greetings to you, too," I said. "In exchange for a large plate of salmon, I'm all yours."

"Follow me." Sorcha checked her customers were happy before leading me behind the counter and into the kitchen. "There's something wrong with my main freezer. It can be glitchy, but my magic usually fixes it. Not this time, though. It keeps switching off, then turning on again, and deep freezing everything. I've even had to throw produce away, since I can't sell it. If I'm not standing beside it all the time monitoring the temperature, it misbehaves."

"How long has this been going on?" I wasn't an expert with electrical devices, but I was aware they malfunctioned around too much magic.

"On and off for a few weeks." Sorcha stood with her hands on her hips. "Maybe it's time for an upgrade. But these things aren't cheap, so I was hopeful I'd get a few more years out of it. Any chance you could look and see if the magic is off?"

I walked from one side of the freezer to the other. It was ticking over, clearly behaving itself while we studied it. "Did Zandra stop by?"

"She did. She wasn't happy," Sorcha said. "I fed her two chocolate chip muffins and two large mugs of coffee with whipped cream and chocolate sprinkles. Oh! And a large butter cookie with frosting."

"She was still miserable after all that sugar and caffeine?"

"More like angry. And I understand why." Sorcha tilted her head as she studied the freezer.

"Is everyone talking about what happened at Randal's house?" I asked.

"The news is spreading faster than a dose of ogre itch after an all-night swingers' party," Sorcha said. "How's Randal doing?"

"He's in shock. Anyone who found their friend dead in the yard and another out cold wouldn't react well." I dabbed a paw on the freezer and swiftly withdrew it.

"Randal is a sensitive guy. I like that about him," Sorcha said. "I'll send him a care package to cheer him up. He's into savory rather than sweet, though. I'll fix him something nice."

"Send it to animal control," I said. "He's not keen on staying in his house at the moment."

"I get that. What a mess. Do the angels have any idea who did it?"

"Not yet. Well, I suppose you've heard the rumor about Zandra's sister, Tempest, being involved?"

Sorcha rested a hand on the freezer and frowned. "Tempest and Wiggles have been mentioned several times. The angels can't be serious about them being cold-blooded killers. There's no way they'd be involved in this murder."

"I'm certain they're not," I said. "But there must be a reason Erick wrote that word in the dirt."

"I heard that whispered about, too. Maybe he panicked and meant to write something else?"

"Whatever's going on, Zandra is unhappy about fingers being pointed at her family. She got furious with Cythera. I told her to take time out and come here, hoping it would help."

"It helped some," Sorcha said, "but Zandra was still in a grump when she left."

"She also argued with Randal," I added. "She blames him for getting the angels involved."

"That's the last thing he needs. I'll send them both food hampers. I was making one anyway, since I've got produce to use up since the freezer so unhelpfully defrosted it. I'll magic them over. That'll distract them from being sad or angry."

"I'm sure it will. Although make sure Zandra gets sweet, not savory." I stepped back from the freezer. "What magic do you use to keep this stable around all the electricity?"

"Balancing spells. They've always done the trick," Sorcha said. "Maybe I should adjust the levels?"

"The magic on this doesn't feel balanced. It feels... icky. It's as if someone has placed some sort of webbing over the doors."

"Like a spider's webbing?" Sorcha wrinkled her nose as she glanced into the corners of the kitchen, as if expecting to see a giant eight-legged critter.

"Touch it. It feels sticky to me."

Sorcha shook her head as she ran her hands over the freezer. "I'm not sensing it. Can you remove it, whatever it is?"

"It should be easy to peel off. Why would anyone want to mess with your freezer, though?"

"To get what's inside?" Sorcha suggested. "I do serve delicious food."

"That, you do. But whoever wants the contents, should order at your counter, not try to steal it from the deep freeze. Give me a minute." I threw out several removal spells until one stuck, then I grabbed the edge and slowly peeled off the sticky magic. Once I yanked off the last piece, I held it in the air for Sorcha to see.

"Oh! That's gross. It's no wonder my freezer keeps malfunctioning if it was covered in that."

"Give me a few minutes, and I'll check the rest of the kitchen. Someone's been messing with you, though." I wandered around the kitchen but found no more of the magic that had covered the freezer. "You're all clear."

"Thanks, Juno. I'll add extra treats to the hamper just for you. And your salmon is on me. I'll just check my other customers are happy and then fix the care package hampers."

Twenty minutes later, with a full belly, and after saying goodbye to Sorcha, I left the café and hurried home. When I arrived, Sorcha's hamper was on the porch, but it was upside down, the contents spilled everywhere. Perhaps her magic was on the fritz. That would explain why the freezer was misbehaving.

I'd just righted the hamper when Zandra blasted out of the front door.

"I was going to meet you at animal control," I said. "I didn't know you were here."

"I got a ping!" she said. "I can get us to Tempest."

"Lead the way."

She scooped me up, cast a translocation spell, and we appeared in a lush woodland.

"Where did the ping bring us?" I peered around at the trees, unfamiliar with our location, although it smelled intensely magical.

"Willow Tree Falls! Tempest must have been here the whole time," Zandra said.

"And she's suddenly letting people know about it?"

"Maybe she wasn't hiding." Zandra set me on the ground and looked around.

"If she wasn't hiding, why was no one able to use a location spell to find her?"

"The magic was misfiring," Zandra said. "The others must have been doing something wrong. Granny Dottie is getting on in years, and magic is harder to control the weaker you get."

"Don't tell Granny Dottie she ever does a spell wrong," I said. "Or you'll find yourself with bright yellow hair and a huge, pus-filled boil on the end of your nose."

"Someone's magic wasn't doing what it was supposed to when we were looking for Tempest," Zandra said. "That's what messed up the spell."

"It wasn't Tempest blocking us?"

"Why would she block us?" Zandra asked. "I found a scarf Tempest left behind when she came to visit, so I used that to cast a spell, and it pointed me here with no trouble."

A high-pitched war cry echoed through the trees, and a second later, something small and heavy landed on me, and a sharp object dug into the back of my neck.

"You're not my usual pony, but I'll take you for a ride. You're in my woods, which means you belong to me. Giddy-up, fluffy pony!"

Whatever strange, foul creature had landed on me blasted out a spell that knocked Zandra over before she could help. Then it dug its heels into my side as if it expected me to start a canter around the trees.

I growled and hissed, sparking out magic, and the sharp object jabbed at me again.

"Behave! This is my land, and that means I own you. If you're no good for riding, then you're no good to me. I'll shove you in a pit and leave you to find out what manner of beasties creep about my wood at midnight."

"Hey! Stop! They're friends. Juno will mess you up if you ride her." Wiggles trotted into view, his usually cheerful demeanor absent, his tail down and his ears droopy.

"They don't have an invitation to come into my woods," the creature on my back said.

"Fallon, stop it! I invited them," Wiggles said. "You remember Zandra, Tempest's sister. That's her familiar, Juno. Stop jabbing her with a spear, or she'll obliterate you. And I won't do anything to stop her."

Fallon let out a derisive snort. "She can try."

"Off! Or I'll smoke you." Wiggles stamped a paw and growled, his eyes glowing red.

The beast on my back huffed and puffed several times before sliding off. "How was I supposed to know? All visitors to these woods go through me. I'm the forest's guardian. And if they don't announce themselves, I can't caution them about the lethal traps in the forest."

"Tempest has warned you about setting those traps. So has Angel Force. You'll get arrested again." Wiggles slumped onto his belly, emitting a gassy belch. "Sorry. My stomach's not been right since the murder accusation started flying around. Juno, Zandra, this is Fallon. She thinks she owns this place, but she's just a guardian of the trees and bushes. You know. Woodland stuff. She takes her responsibilities far too seriously."

Fallon thumped her spear into the dirt, her dark eyes gleaming in the murky light. She was small, solidly built, with nut brown skin. "I do take my responsibilities seriously. If I'm not keeping this place safe, no one is."

"Where's Tempest?" Zandra brushed dried leaves off her jeans as she recovered from being shoved over by Fallon's magic. "I've been looking for her. Everyone has."

"I know! That's why I reached out to you." Wiggles still lay in the dirt.

"That ping was from you?" Zandra asked.

"Yes! I need your help."

"You know Angel Force in Crimson Cove is looking for both of you?" I glared at Fallon, keeping an eye on the spear she waved about.

"Of course I know! They've got us up on that dumb murder charge. Worst idea ever, and those angels have had some stinkers," Wiggles said.

"They just want to talk to you," I said.

Zandra grunted. "I wouldn't be so sure about that. I don't trust Cythera. She had it in for Tempest when she visited over the holidays. She kept questioning her and making her feel uncomfortable."

"Me too," Wiggles said. "I'm still salty because she threw us out of the Christmas party."

"You swam in the cheese fountain!" I said. "And you dunked me in there, too."

"It was glorious," Wiggles said. "But if Cythera's idea of revenge is to put us behind bars for a murder we had nothing to do with, I'll apologize for ruining the fountain of cheese."

"Did Tempest attack Brodie when he found her here?" I asked.

"Brodie? That's the grumpy angel they sent to bring us in?" Wiggles asked.

I nodded. "She could have just disappeared if she didn't want to speak to him."

Wiggles sighed. "I didn't want to attack the guy. He'd done nothing wrong to me, but Tempest demanded I defend her. I didn't think he'd be a problem, but she must have sensed something was off with the guy."

"We always protect our witches," I said. "And I can tell you're worried about Tempest."

Wiggles rolled onto his back and waggled his legs in the air. "Can someone dislodge my gas? All this stress has twisted my guts into a pretzel."

"In exchange for a ride." Fallon sprang into action and pounded on his belly. "That'll get things moving."

Wiggles grunt-farted and waggled his legs some more. "That's got it. I can concentrate now I don't feel like I'm about to explode."

"Talk to us about Tempest," I said. "Why does she need help?"

Wiggles held his breath for several seconds before huffing out smoke. "I thought she was fine. She came back, we talked, and everything seemed normal. But the more I'm around her, I'm realizing she's unstable, and I can't figure out how to fix her."

"Now she's back in Willow Tree Falls, can't your family help?" I asked.

"They would, but they've got their own problems," Wiggles said. "Something's wrong at the demon prison. There was this huge magic malfunction, and a dozen demons escaped. It's all hands on the pump to capture them before they get out of Willow Tree Falls and tear up some innocent town full of non-magicals."

"Is Tempest helping with the recapture?" Zandra asked.

"No. I've got her pinned down, but my magic won't hold her for long."

"You're restraining your witch?" Wiggles must be worried if he was using his magic on Tempest.

"I only trapped her because I needed to talk sense into her, and she wasn't listening to me. She kept jumping to different places and leaving me behind. I can't leave Willow Tree Falls without the right kind of magic wrapped around me, but she always tells me what she's doing. Not anymore. She keeps forgetting about me."

"Let's speak to her," Zandra said. "We need to get to the bottom of this."

Wiggles rolled over, cocked his leg against a tree, and then trotted off.

We followed, with Fallon trailing behind us, yelling to avoid the spiked pits and suspended tree nets.

A few minutes later, we arrived in a woodland clearing. Tempest sat on a tree stump, surrounded by a large shimmer of magic.

"Enough with the games," she said the second she saw Wiggles. Her eyes widened when she spotted us. "Oh! You're here, too. Why?"

"We were worried about you," Zandra said. "What's going on?"

"Wiggles is being weird," Tempest said. "He trapped me here, and he won't tell me why."

I carefully studied Tempest as she spoke to Zandra. She appeared normal, and although she was behind a barrier of magic, I sensed nothing wrong.

"You need to stop hiding from Angel Force," Zandra said. "They think you're involved in Erick's murder."

"I know! But why waste my time with them? I had nothing to do with that guy's death. I'm sorry it happened, but I don't understand why your angels have it in for me."

"You need to speak to them," Zandra said. "And you should apologize to Brodie. You roughed him up something bad. It takes a lot to knock him off his feet."

"He got aggressive toward me! What was I supposed to do, stand there and take it?" Tempest asked.

I leaned in close to Wiggles and kept my voice low. "Why do you think Tempest is unstable? She seems calm enough to me."

"It comes in waves," he whispered back. "She'll be fine for an hour, then she gets this look in her eye, and she's off again."

"And that's not typical behavior?"

"Tempest wants an easy life. We both crave comfort and peace. Her running off to who knows where to do who knows what is strange. I get she has to head off on missions I can't know about sometimes because the angels are secretive about cases, blah-de-blah-confidential-blah. But this is different. Tempest is acting like she no longer cares about anything. She's even ignoring my pups. And no one can ignore those angelic chaos makers for long."

"Come back to Crimson Cove with us and sort this," Zandra said.

Tempest was silent for several seconds. "Do you promise your angels will leave me alone if I do? I don't need the hassle."

"Give them a solid alibi, and you're in the clear. You weren't in Crimson Cove the night Erick was killed and Charlie was injured, were you?"

"Of course not," Tempest said. "Fine. I'll come back and have a boring conversation with your uptight angels. I'll even help you catch the killer if you're struggling. Wiggles, will you get me out of here? You know I can break the magic if I really want to."

"She seems fine," I muttered. "Let's get back to Crimson Cove. Once the angels know Tempest is innocent, they'll back off."

Wiggles stamped his paws a few times and shook out his fur. "I'm telling you, something's wrong. If I let her out, we must watch her. I'm not sure I could use any magic to hurt her, and you might have to if she gets weird again."

I nodded as Wiggles lowered the magic barrier, releasing Tempest. The second he did, I took a step back. On the surface, Tempest seemed normal. She even hugged Zandra. But there was a flicker of something in her eyes. It was there and gone in a second, but it lifted my hackles.

Wiggles was right. Something was grossly wrong. And an unstable Crypt witch could be lethal for all of us.

Chapter 9

Interview gone wrong

The second we stepped into Angel Force with Tempest and Wiggles back in Crimson Cove, it was as if we'd pressed the button to announce World War Witch had begun. The angels sprang into action, their wings flaring and magic dazzling us.

"Relax!" Zandra stepped in front of Tempest. "We come in peace."

"What's going on?" Cythera marched out of her office, carrying a shining blade. Where had she been hiding that?

"Put away your sharp toys," I said. "Tempest and Wiggles are here voluntarily. They didn't need to come, but they want to help."

Cythera's brilliant blue eyes sparked. "Where did you find them?"

"We were home, where we've been this whole time you've been accusing us of being killers," Tempest said. "And just so you know, I can speak for myself."

Wiggles removed his head from a trash can. "So can I."

"You haven't been in Willow Tree Falls. I've had colleagues looking for you over there," Cythera said.

"Then they're lousy at finding things," Tempest said. "I wasn't hiding. I was busy."

"We should take this somewhere private," I suggested. "Cythera, you have questions for Tempest, and she's happy to answer them. And to be crystal clear again, she is here willingly. Tempest wants to help. And she is innocent."

"We'll see about that." Cythera lowered the blade, but it remained in her hand. "We'll use an interview room. Angels, be on alert."

"Why? Is there a fresh round of coffee and donuts being brought in?" Tempest smirked as we headed to the interview room.

"Play nice," Zandra murmured to her. "Cythera has a short temper, even on her best day."

"Mine's pretty short, too," Tempest said. "I'll behave if she does, but I'm not letting some jumped up administrator mess me around and smear the family name."

It took a moment for us to get settled in the interview room, which felt small with us crammed in there. I was on one side of the table, sitting on Zandra's lap with Tempest and Wiggles next to us. Cythera joined us, her blade still close at hand. Finn was also there. And stationed outside the closed interview room door were two angels.

"That's a bit over the top," Zandra muttered, nodding at the angel guards.

"It's protocol. And do we need most of your family in here?" Cythera flicked a cold glance at Zandra.

"I don't keep secrets from my family, so Zandra and Juno are welcome to hear anything we discuss," Tempest said. "If you want to make this official, they're my legal representatives. And I'm not talking if they're kicked out."

Cythera sighed. "I figured you'd say that. Let's hear it then."

Tempest leaned back in her chair. "What do you want to know?"

"Did you kill Erick Farten?"

Cythera was straight in for the kill. This angel wasn't messing around.

"Hand on heart, I had nothing to do with that murder," Tempest said.

"Do you know when Erick died?" Cythera asked.

"I got the relevant information," Tempest said. "After all, you're trying to pin this crime on me, so I needed the facts."

"Where were you on the evening he was killed?"

Tempest hesitated. "On a demon hunt. Don't you know it's my favorite hobby?"

"Where did this hunt take place?"

"Willow Tree Falls."

"If I check with my colleagues in your village, they'll tell me this was a sanctioned hunt?"

"Define sanctioned," Tempest said.

"You should know the definition. You can only legally hunt the demons Angel Force tells you to hunt. If you go after a demon without our permission, you're committing a crime."

"I was hunting. Everyone knew about it. It's no big deal," Tempest said. "And since I was doing the job you angels always fail to achieve, I'm in the clear. Can I go now?"

"No. Tell me your exact movements that evening," Cythera said.

Tempest scratched her forehead. "I'm never good with timings. It's the demons, you see. Some of them mess with your head. They bring chaos and uncertainty. They pump me full of fear, make me forget how powerful I am. It's their way of ruining good times. But I was definitely in Willow Tree Falls. I was too busy to come here and kill a stranger. What would be the point of that?"

"A stranger?" Cythera asked. "You've never met Erick Farten?"

"I didn't know the guy. All I knew was that he was friends with Zandra's boyfriend. And that was only after the guy got himself killed."

"Randal isn't my boyfriend," Zandra muttered. "We work together."

"Whatever label you want to put on it. I didn't know Erick," Tempest said.

Cythera shook her head. "You're lying. We've been running background checks, and we know you've met."

"Not true."

I looked up at Zandra to see if she knew anything about this connection, but she was focused intently on Cythera.

"My checks are accurate," Cythera said.

"They aren't. You've made a mistake," Tempest said.

108

"Did you attend the Henge Valley magic conference two years ago?"

Tempest's forehead furrowed. "Two years ago, you say?"

"Erick was at the conference showcasing new technology to capture demons. His company gave a presentation, and they had a display where his model could be tested. I can confirm that not only did you listen to his presentation, but you also tested the model."

"That doesn't sound like something I'd do." Tempest lifted a finger in the air. "Oh, wait a moment. Was that the conference place with the five-star hotel attached to it? And the all-you-can-eat Chinese buffet next door?"

"I believe so," Cythera said.

"Yes! Then I was there. The five-spice chicken was incredible. I had two plates."

"I remember you telling me about that," Wiggles said. "I still haven't forgiven you for not bringing me back a plate of five-spice."

"Sorry, buddy. It wouldn't have traveled well," Tempest said.

"So, you knew Erick?" A gleam of satisfaction lit Cythera's eyes.

"You've got me. I went to the conference. I don't make a habit of it, but the family takes it in turns to see what's going on. Make connections. Ensure we're not missing any tricks. I don't remember meeting Erick, though."

"You spoke to each other," Cythera said. "And I know Crypt witches aren't fans of new technology."

Tempest tilted her head. "You seem to know a lot about us. Are your sources credible?"

"It pays to monitor complicated covens."

"Complicated?" Tempest drew in a sharp breath. "Are you insulting my family?"

"Move on," I said to Cythera. "Why does it matter that Tempest and Erick were at the same conference two years ago?"

"Because the tech Erick created threatened to take jobs from the Crypt witches."

Tempest snorted. "How exactly are tech nerds threatening my demon hunting skills?"

"A machine instead of a witch capturing demons is more cost-effective," Cythera said. "Less risk of injury or loss of life."

"I guess, if the machine actually worked. I don't remember much about that conference, but I wasn't impressed by what I saw. And I slept through most of the presentations. I have no memory of listening to anyone called Erick Farten. And that's a surname you don't forget."

"But you were there," Cythera said. "And the company Erick worked for recently released a limited-edition model of an electronic demon capture device. It's being trialled by Angel Force."

"Good for them. I hope it's a roaring success," Tempest said. "The fewer demons we have on the streets, the easier life will be for all of us."

"You're not worried about this coming onto the market?" Cythera asked.

"Did you not hear what I just said?"

"You'd be out of work."

"On top of my volunteer demon-capturing job, I have a business that keeps me more than busy," Tempest said. "I wouldn't be worried about having fewer hours to skulk around in the dark after some manky demon who wants to destroy me."

"You sometimes work freelance. That pays well. And I know the other Crypt witches do."

"That's occasional work. And it doesn't make us rich. As Juno said, move on. You're heading toward a dead end and will only look dumb when you have to clumsily back out."

Cythera pressed her lips together. "Why was your name in the dirt underneath Erick's body?"

"We've already cleared that up," I said. "It wasn't Tempest's name. It was just a word. It's not like you to make assumptions."

Cythera scowled at me before focusing on Tempest. "Do you have an explanation?"

"If Erick had put my mugshot next to that word, then I could understand why you're picking on me, but he didn't."

Cythera consulted her notes. "Has Erick or the company he worked for, Dilbert Innovations, ever reached out to you to consult on demon capture techniques?"

"He hasn't, but it happens," Tempest said.

"And what do you do when someone seeks your advice?"

"It depends how big the fee is." Tempest lifted her hands. "Kidding. Before you think I'm getting starry-eyed over money, I make enough not to need extra. These companies are usually full of hot air and only want free advice. I send them packing.

Demon hunting should never become a hobby, which it will if these weird devices get on the mass market. Anyone could pick one up and think they can catch a demon for fun. You'd get groups of teenagers romping around the graveyards in the middle of the night, putting themselves at risk."

"Some would say that was a motive," Cythera said.

"Some people are idiots." Tempest swiped the back of her hand across her forehead. "I didn't know Erick, and I had no issue with him. I can't tell you why he wrote Tempest before he died. It must be a coincidence."

I wasn't big on coincidences, but I kept that worry nugget to myself.

"Are you okay?" Zandra asked Tempest. "If you need to, we can take a break."

"I don't need a break. I just need this over with," Tempest said. "There's a lot going on back home, and I can't afford to be distracted by Angel Force making yet another mess up."

"I heard from my colleague who protects your village that there's been an issue with the demon prison," Cythera said.

"Which is why I should be helping my family, not answering your pointless questions," Tempest said. "We must be done by now."

Wiggles twitched his tail but kept quiet. It was the longest I'd ever heard him stay silent. His furry brow was furrowed, and I was certain he'd cracked a nervous toot once or twice.

"I'm tempted to hold you," Cythera said. "I have good reason. You attacked an angel when he tried to bring you in for questioning."

"That guy has a problem. I was defending myself," Tempest said. "And why send a warrior angel after me?"

"The force assigned to bring you in was reasonable," Cythera said. "You're a powerful witch who wrestles with demons in her spare time. You need a firm hand."

"I need respect and not to be labeled a troublemaker when I've done nothing wrong. He was out of line," she said. "He got mean, so I retaliated."

Wiggles shifted again, clearly uncomfortable with the conversation. Tempest and Wiggles were telling different versions of the same story, and after sensing something was off with Tempest, I was uncertain she was being truthful.

"We could do with some water." Zandra must also be picking up on the discomfort from our side of the table.

"I'm good," Tempest said.

"A few minutes' break," Zandra said. "Everyone's nerves are frazzled."

"If you need it, you can take it," Tempest said.

"We can break. You stay here." Cythera pointed at Tempest. "I'll speak to my colleague in Willow Tree Falls about your demon hunt on the night of Erick's murder." She left the room with Finn.

Zandra turned to Tempest. "Why are you fudging your answers?"

"What do you mean? I told the angels I had nothing to do with Erick's death. That's the truth. I also have no idea why my name was written in the dirt underneath him."

113

"Your alibi could have been clearer. I get that demons mess with your head, but if Angel Force sent you out that evening to capture a problem demon, why not give the full details?"

"Didn't you hear me? Demons are tricksy. They send out twisted magic and spells, so you make mistakes. That night was rough on me. I was given the runaround for hours." Tempest picked at a nail.

"Did you capture the demon?" Zandra asked.

"Hey. What's with all the questions?" Tempest glowered at Zandra. "The way you're talking, it's making me wonder if you think I'm guilty, too."

"I don't! I promise," Zandra said.

"Then act like you're on my side. I came here because you practically begged me to. I want this cleared up and the problem gone as soon as possible."

"So you told the absolute truth?" Zandra asked. "You left nothing out?"

"What would be the point of hiding anything from Angel Force? Eventually, they figure things out. Although they often need a helping hand. Usually from us."

Zandra puffed out a breath. "I'm sorry if you thought I doubted you. Cythera will run her checks, and you'll be free to leave."

"And we will be leaving," Tempest said. "She has no right to hold me. She can try, but I'll bust my way out if I have to."

"Don't mention that's on your mind," Zandra said. "Cythera has zero sense of humor. She'll take it seriously and lock you up out of spite."

"If she tries, I'll break out." Tempest half-smirked. "I know how they love their paperwork, so I could file a few complaints. That'll keep them busy and off my back."

Zandra sighed. "Just... try not to poke the feathered bear. Cythera doesn't play around."

"Neither do I."

Wiggles placed his front paws on the chair and nudged me, gesturing with his head for us to leave the room.

I hopped off Zandra's lap and followed him. He walked all the way to the kitchen, but he wasn't looking for food.

"We have a problem," he said.

"You're worried about Tempest." I kept my voice pitched low. "She's always been sharp, but this feels different."

"It's not just that. When Cythera comes back from checking about the demon hunt, it won't be good news. Tempest went out that evening, but it wasn't on a sanctioned hunt. She was hunting for fun. She told me she got a whiff of something rotten and planned to destroy it."

"Where did she go?"

"I don't know. I couldn't get the information out of her."

I glanced back at the interview room. "Is she hiding something?"

"I hope not." Wiggles scratched behind his ear with a back paw. "Tempest is never this off her game. Her answers are vague, and she's too defensive."

"Do you think she's lying?"

Wiggles looked around to make sure no one could hear us. "Not about Erick, but she's keeping something back. And when Cythera finds out about the unsanctioned hunt, it'll put her in a worse position."

"We need to talk to Tempest. Get her to come clean before Cythera gets wind of this."

Wiggles flicked his tail. "We need to be smart about it. If she clams up, it'll just make things worse."

Cythera rushed out of her office, her wings fluttering and the blade back in her hand.

Uh-oh. It looked like she'd spoken to her angel friend in Willow Tree Falls. Were we too late to undertake damage control?

Chapter 10

Showdown

I tossed out a blocking spell, causing Cythera to walk into an invisible barrier, preventing her from getting to the interview room with her blazing sword and righteously set shoulders.

She bounced off the barrier, landed on her behind, and dropped the blade.

Wiggles snorted a chuckle. "That's one way of doing it. I was thinking of blasting her with a fireball to slow her."

"The angels hate getting their wings singed." I dashed over to Cythera. "What happened? Did you trip over your own feet?"

She grabbed the blade, which was no longer blazing. "Was that you? Who threw out that spell?"

"What's going on?" Zandra slid out of the interview room and shut the door behind her.

"Your fluffy fiend is interfering with law enforcement business," Cythera said. "I should arrest her."

"Juno would never do that," Zandra said. "She makes sure people respect the law. And she has a nose for sniffing out an injustice."

"My wonderful witch is correct, as always," I said. "Cythera, take a moment before charging in and doing something you'll regret."

"You know, don't you?" Cythera said.

"What does Juno know?" Zandra slid me some serious side eye.

"That I intend to hold Tempest until I get the truth out of her," Cythera said.

"Lower your voice! Tempest will be furious if she hears you making threats," Zandra said.

"I have little care about what your devious sister thinks," Cythera said. "I will not be lied to."

"Let's take this into the kitchen," I said. "I spotted a box of cakes in there."

"I can smell them." Wiggles stood beside me. "And I have an explanation for everything. Once you know it all, you won't put Tempest in a cell. You'll most likely give her a medal."

"She deserves the cell. Maybe for the rest of her life," Cythera said.

Finn sidled over. "Cythera, I don't want to interfere, but you need a clear head on this case. You might not like it, but we rely on the Crypt witches to deal with the demons. If they withdraw their support—"

"If they do, we'll handle things," Cythera said. "These witches think we're powerless and have no backbone. They make fun of us."

"Barely. Maybe once a week we say something mildly snide," Wiggles said. "And it's only because you take yourselves too seriously. Lighten up and have fun."

"You're efficient and effective once the correct paperwork is in order." I glanced at Wiggles. "The angels write beautifully on their forms. Lovely penmanship."

Cythera looked furiously vexed at my attempt to compliment her.

"We should at least hear what Wiggles has to say," Finn said. "We don't want the Crypt witches as our enemy."

Cythera huffed and puffed before reluctantly tucking the blade in a concealed holster between her wings. "This had better be good." She stomped into the kitchen.

Zandra scooped me up and settled me on her shoulder. "What's going on? I came out when I heard raised voices."

"Tempest wasn't telling us the complete truth, and Cythera found out."

Zandra sucked in a breath as we followed Cythera, Finn, and Wiggles into the kitchen. "I knew she was hiding something, but she wouldn't say what. Do you know what it is?"

"She went on an unsanctioned demon hunt on the night Erick was murdered. Wiggles said she did it for fun."

"Tempest would never do that. She hunts to keep everyone else safe."

"She would if she's not herself," I said. "You sense it, don't you? Something's wrong with Tempest."

"I... Maybe. She seems different. On the surface, she's fine, but did you see how badly she was sweating during the interview?"

"It's a sign all isn't well."

We stopped our discussion as we reached the kitchen to avoid being overheard.

Cythera was eating a large hunk of chocolate brownie with a white iced top, a clue she was under serious stress, since she usually avoided sugary carbs. Finn picked up a brownie and tossed a vanilla sponge finger to Wiggles.

"I'll make coffee, shall I?" Finn asked.

"No coffee. I want answers," Cythera said. "What do you all know? No more hiding information. If Tempest is guilty, she'll get what's coming to her."

"If you put Tempest in a cell, it'll be the biggest mistake of your career," Zandra said.

"We should hold her. She wasn't on a sanctioned mission the night Erick died. You know it's a crime to hunt a demon without permission," Cythera said.

"She wouldn't have been hunting this demon unless the threat was serious," Zandra said. "Tempest only ever wants to protect people. She must have come across an emergency and dealt with it. Isn't that what happened, Wiggles?"

He made a show of licking crumbs off his muzzle and whiskers. It was a stalling tactic.

"Out with it," Cythera said. "You said you'd explain everything."

"It... yes, it was an emergency situation," Wiggles said with little confidence. "Sometimes, we have to act first and seek permission afterward. Demons don't always wait for the paperwork to be signed off before committing their evil deeds."

"What devious demon needed hunting so urgently?" Cythera asked. "My colleague in Willow Tree Falls had no alerts on her desk."

"Then her paperwork is out of date," I said. "There are a number of demons currently loose from the prison."

"That's under control," Cythera said. "They're being hunted by the prison guardians. Your family." She looked at Zandra.

"Tempest would never do anything bad," Wiggles said. "You have to trust her."

"She's a good witch," I said.

"Tempest is a messed up demon slayer who spends most of her time with troublemakers. Darkness can spread. It's corrupted her," Cythera said.

"The family deals with darkness daily, but they do it for the right reasons. They've saved magical communities countless times. Show some flexibility with Tempest," I said. "She had to stop an injustice from happening."

"Yeah, what Juno says," Wiggles said hurriedly. "That's what happened. Tempest is a heroine. She probably saved the world, and all you want to do is bring trouble to her door."

It didn't feel right to keep information from Cythera and Finn. I was concerned about Tempest's stability. Wiggles had revealed Tempest was troubled and had gone off hunting for fun, but if they knew that, it would make matters worse. And if they attempted to put Tempest in a cell, the outcome would be grim for any angel who got in her way.

It was better to keep this information back and gather the relevant details. I could present it all to Cythera once the murderer had been found. Perhaps she'd charge Tempest for going on an illegal hunt, but better that than being charged with murder.

"I have a solution to you shoving an angry Crypt witch into a cell," I said. "You have concerns about Tempest because she may have concealed a tiny amount of information. That doesn't make her a killer, though."

"She outright lied!" Cythera said. "There was no authorized hunt on the night of the murder. If she's lied about that, what else has she lied about?"

"Tempest was in Willow Tree Falls that night," Wiggles said. "I'll vouch for her."

"You'd say anything to protect your witch," Cythera said. "Your word means nothing to me."

Wiggles growled at her.

I continued before Wiggles took a chunk out of Cythera. "My solution is, Tempest and Wiggles stay with us until this matter is resolved."

Zandra nodded swiftly. "We have the space. And Vorana won't mind two extra house guests. And she already knows them."

"Can you control her?" Cythera asked.

"There's nothing to control," Zandra said. "I trust Tempest with my life."

That thought sent a shiver all the way to the tip of my tail. I wasn't sure I did. Not with the way she was behaving.

"It's a great idea," Finn said. "We keep Tempest close by while we do follow-up research. Why put her behind bars when there's an easier option? A safer option."

"Because I don't trust Tempest," Cythera said. "She worries me."

"Worry less about Tempest and focus on finding out who killed Erick, attacked Charlie and put him in a coma, and knocked out Randal with a powerful spell," I said. "If you focus your resources on Tempest and you've got the wrong person—which you absolutely have—this will be a waste of time. What if the killer strikes again while you're looking for evidence you'll never find?"

Cythera pressed her lips together. "Very well. Tempest stays in Crimson Cove. If she leaves town, I'll arrest her. That goes for you, too." She looked down at Wiggles.

"I can't stay for too long," Wiggles said. "I'm in a magic bubble, you see. It's the only thing keeping me alive. If I'm away from Willow Tree Falls, I don't do so good."

"We can work on that," I said. "I'll keep your magic topped up so you can stay with Tempest. She'll want you by her side."

"I'm happy to work with your magic." Wiggles wagged his stubby tail and nodded a thanks at me.

"Tempest won't be happy about us making these decisions about her freedom," Zandra muttered to me.

"She won't, but a cozy stay with Vorana is better than being stuck in a cell while she curses the angels," I said.

"Tempest is your responsibility," Cythera said, hammering the point home. "If this goes wrong, I'm coming after you, and you'll be charged with accessory to murder."

"And we'll welcome you with open paws if we're hiding a killer," I said.

Five minutes later, with a grumbling Tempest in tow and Wiggles trotting beside her, we hurried out of Angel Force before Cythera changed her mind.

"What were you playing at back there?" Zandra asked Tempest the second we were clear of angel ears.

"Nothing! Get off my back. You've been hanging out with angels too much. You even have their cinnamon stink."

"Why did you tell Cythera you were on a sanctioned demon hunt the night of the murder? She uncovered the truth with a single call."

"It's no big deal. I'll sweet talk the Willow Tree Falls feathers, and they'll rustle up the right paperwork to get me off the hook."

Zandra scowled. "Was there even a demon?"

"Sure. I sensed a problem was on the prowl, so I dealt with it. Sometimes, waiting for the green light from Angel Force takes too long."

"You said you didn't catch anything," Zandra said.

"I did my best. We can't all be as perfect as you." Tempest increased her stride. "I don't want to talk about this."

"You need to get your story straight." Zandra hurried after her, and I walked behind with Wiggles, a swirl of unease unsettling my stomach.

"Tempest, talk to me!" Zandra said.

"I'm done talking. All I want to do is grab some food and crash."

"Tempest must be hungry," Wiggles said. "I'm the same. If my stomach so much as grumbles, that's it. I can't think about anything else, and I snap at everyone. All I can focus on is food."

"Let's hope it's that simple to solve." I had a bad feeling this problem was more than an empty stomach, but I was glad we'd gotten Tempest away from the angels to give them all breathing space and time to cool down.

Once we were back at Vorana's house, Zandra explained the situation. Vorana was happy to have two extra house guests and agreed they could use the guest bedroom, though Tempest was content in the basement with us. And so was I, since I wanted to keep a close eye on her.

While Tempest and Zandra were in the basement, sorting spare bedding and moving things around, I headed back up the stairs and into the kitchen. Vorana was making snacks, while Sage sat in her seat half-asleep. Wiggles stood beside Vorana, begging for food.

"Thank you for helping at such short notice," I said.

"I like Tempest," Vorana said. "I'm sorry she's in the middle of this muddle. I'm hoping these snacks will put a smile on her face."

"They are mine," Wiggles said. "And I'm sure I can smell something meaty roasting."

"You can, and you'll get your share when it's ready, but that's for later," Vorana said. "Help yourself to Sage's treats in the bowl over there if you can't wait."

"If you touch my treats, you'll be sorry," Sage grumbled, eyes still closed.

While Wiggles went off to investigate the treats, much to a hissing Sage's disgust, I jumped up close to Vorana. "I'm sure Tempest will behave but keep an eye on her. There's something not right about this mystery."

"If there's any problem, Sage has my back," Vorana said. "You get on and solve this murder. I'll make sure our guests are occupied."

"Thank you again. That's exactly what we intend to do."

Fifteen minutes later, Zandra and I made our excuses, saying we had an appointment, and slipped out of the house, leaving Tempest stuffing in the snacks on the couch next to Wiggles.

"We need to find out more about Erick," I said. "We'll spend the afternoon at animal control, catching up on jobs, but then we'll head to Erick's office and speak to his colleagues. There could be someone who knows what happened to him."

"Ugh! You're going to surround me with tech geeks, aren't you?" Zandra wrinkled her nose.

"Is your fondness for tech geeks fading?" I asked.

"Have I ever had a fondness for them?"

"I know you do. One in particular."

"If you mean Randal, I'm not talking to him."

"He is sorry about everything," I said. "He was so panicked after discovering his friend was dead and another injured that he wasn't thinking clearly when he showed up with Brodie."

Zandra sighed. "I don't blame him, but he jumped to the same conclusions as the angels. Why does everyone think Tempest is bad?"

"Not everyone does. But remember, she spent most of her life battling a troublesome demon trapped inside her. She's got him under control, thanks to you and Aurora, but memories linger. He was a chaos-maker and led Tempest into mischief."

"People also forget that the demon sometimes helped."

"A demon never helps unless it's for his own benefit," I said. "You told me the stories, so I know what a troublemaker he was."

"But he sometimes lent Tempest power, and he even helped bring back Wiggles."

"And left behind a few gassy, pungent side-effects," I said. "Reputations stick, and they're hard to shift. Gossip is always more fun when it's about someone misbehaving."

"So, because of people's narrow-mindedness, my sister is being accused of a crime she didn't commit?"

"I'm as sure as you that Tempest didn't kill Erick," I said, "but she isn't being honest, and that's worrying."

"She'll have her reasons," Zandra said. "Maybe she messed up on the demon hunt and is embarrassed the demon got away."

"Why cover that up when she knows the angels are looking at her for murder?"

"You don't know my sister like I do. She's even more stubborn than me."

"Is that possible?"

"You bet it is." Zandra lifted me up. "I don't know what's going on with Tempest, but we need to focus on clearing her name. All other problems can wait."

Chapter 11

Business talk

The building we stood outside of was twelve stories high, with a sleek, modern design, topped with a substantial set of slanted solar panels.

"I'm not a fan of the city," Zandra said, wrinkling her nose.

I scooted my tail out of the way as someone rushed past, nearly stepping on it. "Everyone is in their own head, thinking only of their business and not looking outward. But cities have their own stark beauty."

"We always make time for each other in Crimson Cove," Zandra said. "I get the impression people who live in a place like this rush around just to look busy and impressive. I'm surprised Erick worked at a place like this. He was like Randal. And he hates the city."

"Maybe Erick could work remotely, like Randal does," I said. "He's always doing jobs to help with magic wards or fixing tech glitches in other locations. Randal could live anywhere he wanted, but he set up a base in Crimson Cove to be close to you."

Zandra looked away. "He didn't do it for that reason."

"I'm glad he did. Randal makes working at animal control far more interesting. I'm sure you agree."

"Not at the moment, I don't."

"Let's go inside and see what Erick's boss has to say about him," I said. "We should speak to some of his colleagues, too, get to know Erick better and uncover any dark secrets he was keeping that got him killed."

After convincing the angels that Tempest and Wiggles were safe with us, we'd swiftly arranged a visit to Dilbert Innovations. Erick's boss, Dilbert Dimitri, had a free slot that afternoon, so we'd hot-pawed it over here after finishing work at animal control.

We entered the building, which was starkly modern, with minimal furniture in the lobby, white walls, marble flooring, and a pristine white reception desk. We announced ourselves, got directions to the right floor, then headed to a large glass elevator.

Zandra peered over the edge as we zoomed skyward then quickly backed away. "They must have some serious magic wards around all this electricity. What if this thing glitches? We'd plummet to our deaths."

"That's what this company is so skilled at doing," I said. "If Erick was half as talented as Randal, he would have no trouble ensuring there are no death doom plummets."

"Even so, let's get off this thing quickly, just in case things aren't as stable as they appear."

A minute later, the doors pinged and opened smoothly, leading us into another reception area. A smartly dressed woman with a blonde pixie cut and red-framed glasses sat at the reception desk, greeting us with a smile.

"You're here to see Mr. Dimitri?" she asked.

Zandra nodded and introduced us.

"He's available now. Follow me." She led us into a fancy office unlike the rest of the building we'd seen so far, dominated by wood and warm lighting. Mr. Dimitri stood by the floor-to-ceiling window, his hands behind his back. He wore a dark, expensive-looking suit, although the baseball cap perched on his head was an interesting addition. He also wore sneakers.

Mr. Dimitri turned from the window, striding over and nodding in greeting. He looked around fifty, well-preserved, some might even say handsome, with a gleam of intelligence in his dark eyes.

"Sylvia, it's time for coffee. Would you like to join me?" he asked us.

Zandra nodded, but I declined.

We settled into seats as Mr. Dimitri returned to his desk.

"I heard the terrible news about Erick. Everyone is in shock. He was well-liked in the company."

"Where did you hear about his death?" I asked.

"We have top-of-the-line technology that scours news sources," Mr. Dimitri said. "We have alerts set up for anything that mentions this company or our employees. Someone on my team sent me the information in the early hours of the morning. Of course, I didn't see it right away. You're involved in the investigation?"

"We work freelance with Angel Force when there's a complicated case to pursue," I said.

"What's complicated about what happened to Erick?" Mr. Dimitri asked.

"The way he died is unusual," I said. "Initial inquiries have provided us with no obvious suspects."

"Suspects? This wasn't an accident or a natural death?"

"Magic killed him," Zandra said. "It appears Erick was running away from his attacker when it happened."

"I... goodness. I see. Erick was incredible with magical technology. He was always coming up with new ideas and inventing things. But his natural magic needed a nudge. If he didn't have some kind of equipment to channel his energy through, he was weak. I suppose, if he'd been caught unawares, he wouldn't have been able to defend himself." Mr. Dimitri leaned back. "But who would do this to him? And Charlie, too. Both of them were excellent employees. The sort of men you could never imagine getting into trouble."

"That's why we're investigating," I said. "Could you tell us more about Erick? What was he like to work with?"

"He was excellent. Hard-working. Dedicated. A quiet man, though. Sometimes, I wished I had more employees like Erick. He could get overexcited about a new idea rather than finishing an old one, but he was smart and had a passion for what he did. He wasn't in it for the money. He was in it for his love of creating new technology to help people. These days, that's a rare find."

"It sounds as if you liked him," Zandra said.

"I liked his results. I won't say he was popular. You get a lot of loners who like to invent. They get lost in their own worlds, caught up in their heads, and leave people out—or tread on toes to get what they want. But Erick had an excellent friendship with Charlie. They worked well together."

"How long did Erick work for you?" I asked.

"He started out as a freelancer, but I quickly saw his talent and brought him on board full-time. I'd say he's been here at least three years, possibly longer, but I'd have to check the records. He was doing such a good job that I was considering offering him a promotion. We like to hold on to talent when we can."

Sylvia appeared with the coffee and handed it around. She glanced at me, and there was a flash of worry in her eyes. Had she overheard something she didn't agree with?

"Thank you, Sylvia. That'll be all," Mr. Dimitri said.

She hurried out, slowing as she closed the door, making eye contact with me again.

"Did Erick have enemies?" Zandra asked. "Any problems with other colleagues?"

"He mainly kept to himself." Mr. Dimitri stirred his coffee. "I know all wasn't well with his family. Have you spoken to them?"

"Not yet," I said.

"He had a small family. His parents aren't alive, I believe, but there are siblings. He didn't talk about them, but I got the impression he'd grown up with very little. Most likely they come from the wrong side of the tracks. He left them behind and made a name for himself."

"Did they ever visit Erick at work?" I asked. "Cause problems?"

"No, nothing like that. He barely spoke about his family, and when he did, there was tension, and he was keen to change the subject. Every year, we have a big summer party for employees' families to come to, and I said he could bring anyone he liked. He said none of his family were free, and it wasn't their sort of thing, anyway." Mr. Dimitri sighed. "We don't all get along with our families, do we? We can't choose which family we're born into. And blood isn't always best."

"This is just a formality, but could you tell us your alibi for the night Erick died?" Zandra asked.

"You're being thorough, aren't you?" Mr. Dimitri lowered his coffee. "I'm no killer."

"We need to check everyone close to Erick."

A flicker of irritation stirred to life. "I'm a slave to my work. It's my one true love. I'd have been working here that evening. I'm here late most nights. It's both a blessing and a curse to have turned my passion into my career. I never want to stop tinkering."

"Erick died in the early hours of the morning—around midnight, possibly later," I said. "Do you really work that late?"

"It's not uncommon. When we're in the middle of an intense project, we often pull all-nighters. Even the boss doesn't get out of those." Mr. Dimitri pointed behind us. "That couch turns into a comfortable pullout bed, which I've used many times. I'm certain I was here but check with Sylvia. She knows my calendar inside and out. That'll set your minds at ease."

"Thank you. We appreciate the help," Zandra said.

Mr. Dimitri downed his coffee. "I am sorry to rush you, but I've got a mountain of work to get through. If I can be of any more help, please get in touch."

We left the office, and I hopped onto the reception desk, startling Sylvia. "Greetings! I believe you'd like to talk to us."

Her eyes widened before her gaze darted to the closed door. "Not here! Meet me at Café Pastel in half an hour. It's five minutes from here. You can't miss it. It's got a huge red and pink sign."

I nodded, leapt onto Zandra's shoulders, and directed her toward the elevator.

"What was that about?" Zandra asked.

"I believe the nosy secretary has something she needs to tell us."

Half an hour later, Zandra was finishing a hot chocolate, and I had a rather unimpressive dried fish stick I'd abandoned in disgust. Posh coffee shops could often be a disappointment, trading on the name rather than the quality of their food.

Sylvia hurried in, looked around, and spotted us. She placed an order at the counter then dashed over, glancing around before perching on the edge of a chair. "There's no one in here I know. That's good. Thank you for waiting."

"You're welcome. I could tell there was something on your mind," I said.

"I need to be careful," Sylvia said. "If I get caught, I'll lose my job."

"Are you doing something wrong by talking to us?" Zandra asked.

We waited as a large coffee was brought over to Sylvia, along with a plate of brownies.

"Help yourself," she said once the server had left. "I always find courage when I eat chocolate."

Sylvia and Zandra tucked in while I waited with as much patience as I could muster.

"Did you know Erick well?" I asked.

Sylvia nodded. "I admired him. I couldn't believe it when I heard what happened to him. I burst into tears in front of the whole department. It was embarrassing."

"You admired him, or were you sweet on him?" Zandra asked.

Sylvia sighed. "I cared for Erick more than I should. I knew better than to fall for someone with an obsessive passion for his career. Most of the people who work at the company are the same. The only thing they love is their inventions. Erick was no different. But he was funny. I liked his dad joke humor. And he often brought me devices to test when Mr. Dimitri wasn't around. Erick seemed interested in my thoughts."

"Did he ever ask you out?" I asked.

"No. Well, he made comments sometimes that made me think he wanted more. And he liked to touch my arm. Well, he sort of stroked it. Erick always stroked my arms when I wore silk."

"You didn't find that creepy?" Zandra asked.

Sylvia pushed her glasses up her nose. "When you're not brilliant or beautiful, you take what you're given. And no, I didn't find it creepy. I get lonely, same as everyone. Erick paid me attention."

"Everyone we've talked to said he was clever," I said.

"Erick was a genius. So smart. He designed the magic drying cloth. A hair serum that cured cow licks, and an ever-heating mug. Those were just some of the products he sold to non-magicals. He was always able to find the right balance of magic to slip into an invention so it could be safely used."

"He liked helping non-magicals?" I asked.

"I'm not sure he had a preference, but that's where the massive amounts of money are. Magic users don't always need magical tech, but non-magicals benefit from it, yet they don't even know what they're using."

"It sounds like Erick made this company a lot of money," Zandra said.

"That's why I needed to talk to you." Sylvia paused and looked around again. "I do everything for Mr. Dimitri. From fixing his messy paperwork to booking the company's accommodation. When I heard Mr. Dimitri say he was planning on promoting Erick, I knew he was lying. Erick was underpaid and exploited."

"Aren't people with Erick's skills in high demand?" I asked.

"Yes! But Erick wasn't a people person. Some thought he was rude or pushy."

"We may have experienced that," I said. "He wasn't subtle in his overtures to Zandra."

"Erick asked you on a date?" Sylvia's mouth dropped open.

"No! He was just clumsy with how he approached me."

Sylvia sniffed. "It was just him! He meant no harm, but it meant other people didn't want to work with him. He sort of got stuck here."

"And Mr. Dimitri made the most of Erick's social awkwardness?" I asked.

"He knew exactly what he was doing. Mr. Dimitri doesn't come from a magical tech background. He used to be in corporate finance. He did that thing where they'd buy badly performing companies, strip out the profitable bits, sell them, and get rid of the rest, leaving hundreds of people without jobs. He moved into this industry because he saw the insane amounts of money that could be made when magical tech was slipped into non-magical communities. Erick's self-heating mug has made the company billions. It's cheap to make and has huge profit margins."

"I'm still uncertain how Erick was being exploited," Zandra said. "He seemed happy in his work."

"Erick loved his tech toys, and as long as someone provided the space and opportunities to explore, he was happy. His problem was, he often forgot to file the patent paperwork. He was also terrible at finishing projects. He'd make things almost perfect then get bored. That meant Mr. Dimitri could pick it up, finesse it, and sell it. The same goes with the patents. If Erick didn't file them, Mr. Dimitri did."

"What did Erick have to say about that?" I asked.

"He barely noticed. And if he did, Mr. Dimitri talked him around." Sylvia paused for breath and for a bite of brownie. "On one occasion, I caught Mr. Dimitri snooping around Erick's desk. He hid some paperwork inside his jacket. Then he caught me looking and made me promise to keep silent. He bought me expensive gifts in an attempt to bribe me. And guess what happened?"

"I'm uncertain, but intrigued," I said.

"He sold the design he stole to another company for a massive amount of money. Erick was stunned, but Mr. Dimitri convinced him they'd simply had the same idea at the same time. Which was impossible, because Mr. Dimitri is half as smart as Erick."

"But Erick was convinced that's what happened?" I asked.

"Erick was genius-level smart when it came to tech, but naïve with everything else. He barely questioned people's motives." Sylvia swirled what was left of her coffee. "I saw Mr. Dimitri steal the designs from Erick's desk. He profited from Erick's messiness and naivete."

"It's an incredible motive for murder," I said.

"That's why I had to tell you. I heard how Erick died, so I knew it wasn't an accident."

"Mr. Dimitri gave us an alibi for the time of Erick's murder," I said. "He said to check it with you. Apparently, he was pulling an all-nighter at the office on the night of the murder."

Sylvia pulled a small device with a flat screen from her purse and scrolled down it with her fingers. "He was scheduled to work late that night, but I left at six o'clock, so I can't be sure if he stayed. And he works alone, so it's unlikely anyone on the tech floor saw him. They're a floor down from the executive offices."

"Mr. Dimitri could have been worried Erick knew he'd stolen his design," Zandra said. "He silenced Erick before he could ruin his career."

"There's one way to know for sure what Mr. Dimitri was up to that night," Sylvia said. "You need to speak to Lucinda."

"His wife?" I asked.

Sylvia smirked. "Oh, he's married, but Lucinda is his mistress."

Chapter 12

Spicy dinner

After our intriguing meeting with Sylvia and learning Mr. Dimitri had not only a wife but a lady friend on the side, we decided to dig for dirt. Sylvia had returned to work but let us know Mr. Dimitri was scheduled for another late-night work session, although had also booked a table at an expensive restaurant not far from the office.

Which was why we'd lurked in the café, eating overpriced food and waiting for the offices to empty for the evening. As people started walking past in their suits, purposefully marching home and away from the office drudge, we left the café and headed back to Dilbert Innovations.

We were only waiting a few minutes before Sylvia emerged, dressed in a deep red button up coat and carrying her large purse. She was closely followed by Mr. Dimitri, who appeared to be pursuing her.

"Has he found out Sylvia's been revealing his secrets?" I was ready to spring into action if Mr. Dimitri caused Sylvia trouble.

"I'm not sure he's chasing her," Zandra said. "If he is, she's not worried about being followed by him."

I cocked my head. "Perhaps they're the ones having an affair. They spend a lot of time together."

Zandra glanced up from her mobile snow globe. "Are they making it look like they're leaving separately? If so, they're doing a terrible job. We spotted them straight away."

"Office romances are difficult to hide," I said. "Everyone knows everyone else's business. It's just like living in a small community."

"Crimson Cove isn't so small, and everyone knows our business." Zandra scowled at her mobile snow globe. "I can't get a reply from Tempest or Vorana. I wanted to make sure there were no problems at home."

"If there were problems, Vorana would have let us know," I said. "And Sage would never let anything bad happen. We did the right thing by offering Tempest and Wiggles a place to stay while we solve this crime."

Zandra sighed and shoved her mobile snow globe into her back pocket. "I'm worried about Tempest, though. She hates to admit to any weakness, but she must be sick with something. She's never usually that sweaty. It was gross. I could smell the sweat when Cythera interviewed her."

"And she's used to being around angels, so that wouldn't have bothered her," I said. "We'll get to the bottom of it. Look! They're going in different directions. Let's follow Mr. Dimitri. See what he's up to."

Zandra grunted. "So much for him having a late-night work session. Typical higher-up. Leave all the hard work to everybody else."

"Isn't that what they're supposed to do?" I asked. "The big boss gets the big bucks for ordering people around."

"From what I saw of Mr. Dimitri and Sylvia's relationship, she keeps him in order. She should get the bigger salary."

I hopped onto Zandra's shoulder, and we continued following Mr. Dimitri. He led us away from the business district and along a road lined with restaurants. There was every kind of cuisine you could imagine, from Chinese to Mexican. I did my best not to drool on Zandra's shoulder, but the smells drifting out of these restaurants were glorious. Meaty. Rich. Fragrant.

Mr. Dimitri stopped outside a Japanese restaurant. He checked his appearance in the glass, adjusted his tie, then headed inside. We remained outside, keeping out of his sightline as we pretended to inspect the laminated menu stuck in the window.

"He's meeting a lady," I said.

"His wife or his mistress?" Zandra muttered.

"There was a picture of a woman on his desk in the office," I said. "That's not her."

"The mistress, then," Zandra said.

"She's attractive. I'd say at least fifteen years younger than Mr. Dimitri."

"I expect his wife is at home, thinking he's working hard, when instead, he's playing away." Zandra shook her head. "From what we're learning about Mr. Dimitri, he's an all-around bad guy. He exploits his staff and cheats on his wife. What else has he done?"

"He lied to us about his alibi for the night of Erick's murder," I said.

"Shady. Not to be trusted. Possibly a killer."

We lurked for ten minutes. A waiter took their order, and a bottle of champagne was brought over. The woman dining with Mr. Dimitri appeared delighted and jumped up to kiss his cheek. She grabbed her purse and headed to the back of the restaurant, giving him a little finger wave.

"Now's our chance to talk to Lucinda," I said. "If she's off to powder her nose, we can corner her."

"We can't go through the restaurant," Zandra said. "Mr. Dimitri will see us, and he'll figure out we're following him. We don't want to make him suspicious, or he might run."

"Then we'll go around the back and through the kitchen," I said.

It took us a few seconds to find the alleyway that led to the back of the restaurants, but we quickly located the access door to the Japanese restaurant and snuck inside. We didn't have to go through the kitchen, but instead followed a stark white corridor. There was an entrance and exit door leading into the kitchen, but we went the other way, heading toward the restaurant sounds.

Zandra found the restroom, and we headed inside. Mr. Dimitri's lady friend was washing her hands. She glanced up at us as we entered and smiled. "I like your cat."

"And I like those diamonds in your earlobes," I said. "A gift from an admirer?"

"Oh! You're a talker. You can never tell, can you?" Lucinda said. She applied a fresh coat of red lip gloss.

"I am indeed a talker," I said. "And I'd be interested in talking to you."

Lucinda's pretty, dark eyes slid my way. "What about?"

"We're interested in how you know Mr. Dimitri," Zandra asked.

Lucinda snapped the lid back on her lip gloss and popped it inside her tiny black purse. "How do you know him?"

"That's what I asked you," Zandra said. "You seem close."

"What if we are?"

"Then we're interested in learning more," I said. "And answering a question with a question creates circles you can never untwist from."

Lucinda huffed out a breath. "I don't know you, and I don't have to answer your questions."

"It would be in your best interest if you did." Zandra made a show of blocking the door and folding her arms over her chest. "We're looking for information. You may be able to help us."

Lucinda turned to face us. "Did she send you?"

"Who would *she* be?" I asked.

"If you know Dilbert at all, then you'll know he's married. And not to me."

"We assumed as much," I said.

She huffed out a breath. "Who are you? Deadbeat private investigators, I suppose?"

"We're neither deadbeat nor private about anything," I said and swiftly made the introductions.

Lucinda nodded. "I know what she's like. She doesn't trust him."

"Having witnessed your dinner date so far, I can see why," I said.

Lucinda fidgeted with the strap of her revealing dress. "I don't want trouble."

"Yet it's found you," Zandra said. "All we want to do is talk, and then we'll leave you alone."

"What has the good little wife told you to do to me?" Lucinda asked.

"Nothing bad." I played along in the hope she'd talk if she thought Dilbert's wife had sent us to spy on her. "But we do need information from you about Mr. Dimitri."

"Information about what? His wife knows everything about him. I'm certain she snoops through his messages and checks his pockets. It's embarrassing."

"Does she know about his extramarital activities?" I asked.

"Well, not for certain, but she knows he's up to something he shouldn't be," Lucinda said. "She must know about me, since she sent you to scare me off."

"Let's make a deal," I said. "We won't mention seeing you with Mr. Dimitri this evening if you answer our questions."

"How do I know you're telling the truth?" Lucinda asked.

"You don't, but we're not interested in your affair," Zandra said. "We think Mr. Dimitri is up to no good, and we need to know why. He could be in serious trouble."

Lucinda hesitated. "Oh! That's different. I'm confused. Who sent you? What trouble is he in?"

"We work freelance," I said. "The highest bidder usually wins. Unfortunately, we have strict client confidentiality rules, so we can't share more information with you. But you have our word, we won't reveal what we learned about your relationship with Mr. Dimitri to his wife. All we ask in return is information. That sounds reasonable, doesn't it?"

"I... I suppose. What do you want to know? Make it quick. I need to get back to the table. I have a glass of bubbly waiting."

"How long has your affair been going on?" I asked.

"Six months," Lucinda said. "I go to a bar near here because it's where the top business types drink. It's a great place to pick up guys. The kind of guys I like, anyway."

"Older, richer, and already attached?" Zandra asked.

Lucinda flashed her a sharp smile. "We all have our preferences. I like sugar daddies. They're fun. And I only ever get involved with other women's husbands. I don't want the drudgery that comes with having an actual husband. Once they have a ring on your finger, they get boring. All the promises of vacations, gifts, a life of luxury—it all goes. That's not for me. I wasn't born clever, and I had to fight to get where I am using the only assets I have." She pointed to her face and then her chest. "I'm making the most of these before they're gone and drooping toward my knees."

There was a light tap on the restroom door, and a second later, Mr. Dimitri appeared, a sly smile on his face.

I could tell what he was here for. He thought he'd have some slap and tickle in the restroom before the main course arrived. Dessert before dinner.

His expression froze when he saw us, but before he backed away, Zandra yanked him into the restroom and slammed the door.

"What is the meaning of this?" Mr. Dimitri attempted to free himself from Zandra's grip, but she flared magic around her fist, and he was unable to escape.

"We're speaking to your charming lady friend," I said. "And what a surprise to find you here. Weren't you planning on working late again?"

Mr. Dimitri spluttered for a few seconds before regaining a fraction of composure. "I... well, everyone needs to eat. There's nothing wrong with me having dinner with a friend."

"This isn't an affair?" I asked. "You didn't buy those diamond earrings for Lucinda and the expensive champagne? Or do you usually treat friends so well?"

"How I treat my friends is none of your damned business." The pleasant attitude we'd encountered earlier was gone as Mr. Dimitri realized he'd been caught with his pants down.

"Do you usually visit your friends while they're in the restroom?" Zandra asked.

"I was worried! Lucinda had been gone for some time. I needed to make sure she wasn't unwell," Mr. Dimitri said.

Zandra released her grip on him and shoved him back. "You're cheating on your wife. And when we questioned you, you lied about where you were."

"I told you the truth about Erick. That's the most important thing."

"Erick! Is that what this is about?" Lucinda asked. "What's Erick gone and done now? He's such a sleaze. Always grabbing at me with those clammy hands. Some irritated woman finally reported him, I suppose?"

"Erick is dead," I said. "That's why we're here. We need to find out what happened to him, and we think your sugar daddy is involved."

Lucinda's eyes widened, and her gaze flashed to Mr. Dimitri. "Did you know about this?"

"They asked me questions this afternoon," he said. "Of course, I heard the news earlier. And as I explained, I have no information about what happened or who did this to Erick."

Lucinda squeaked. "Did this? This was murder?"

"Why are you bothering Lucinda about this?" Mr. Dimitri slid over to Lucinda and placed a protective hand on her waist. "She knows nothing."

"Because we're checking your alibi," I said. "You said you were working late, but that wasn't true. You weren't at the office, so where were you? Visiting Crimson Cove to commit murder?"

"I'm disgusted you doubt my word," Mr. Dimitri said. "I'm a respectable businessman."

"And I'm disgusted you're cheating on your wife," Zandra said. "Where were you on the night Erick died?"

"Working!"

Lucinda rested a hand on Mr. Dimitri's chest. "Erick had the social skills of a startled toad, but I'd never want him dead. He'd blush whenever I spoke to him. It was kind of cute."

"You've met him?" I asked.

"A few times. Erick was always beavering away on some project. He gave me a free sample of hair serum once. That stuff worked miracles." Lucinda blinked big, innocent eyes at me. "You can't think my Dilbo is a killer. He's a lover, not a fighter, if you know what I mean."

"Do you know his recent movements?" I asked. "Has he been working late this week?"

She smiled coyly. "That depends on who you ask. Ask his wife, and she'd say yes. Ask me, and I'd say we've been together every evening this week. As I told you, we've been a couple for six months, so we had a big anniversary to celebrate. We went to the theater and had some yummy dinners. Later on this evening, we're going to a cabaret. He always spoils me."

"You were together every evening?" I asked.

Lucinda beamed. "I insisted on it if he wants to keep me all to himself. A whole week of celebrating. I got these diamonds on the first night. I've never felt so spoiled and special."

Mr. Dimitri's cheeks grew pink. "The only reason I told you I was at the office was to avoid complicating things. I don't want my private life dug into. You had no right to come after Lucinda."

"We had every right, since we need to solve Erick's murder," I said.

Mr. Dimitri threw up his hands. "If anyone killed Erick, it was a member of his family! I already told you they're difficult people. Pester them and leave us alone. Come on, Lucinda. Our food is waiting."

They left the restroom, the door thumping closed behind them.

"What do you think about that?" Zandra asked.

"If they were wining and dining and seeing shows all week, darling Dilbo couldn't have vanished to murder Erick."

"We can get Finn to check receipts and restaurants, but I reckon he's in the clear."

"It's disappointing. His motive was excellent."

Zandra nodded. "At least that's one liar ticked off the list."

"It's progress. Tomorrow, we'll talk to Erick's family. See what skeletons we can unearth from the closets."

Chapter 13

Family ties

"You'll miss breakfast if you don't get up." I nudged Sage with a paw, but she refused to open her eyes.

"She's been so sleepy recently." Vorana stood by the stove, a wooden spoon dangling from one hand. Although she wasn't paying attention to the bacon crisping, she was looking out the window. "Me too. No matter how long I sleep, I don't want to get out of bed. It was a real effort this morning."

"I'll eat your breakfast if you don't move," I said to Sage.

She barely twitched a muscle. It was unlike Sage not to be interested in breakfast. We'd often compete to be the first in our chairs at the table.

"The kittens will do that for her. They've been so naughty." Vorana squeaked and dashed over as smoke billowed from the toaster. She yanked out two charred slices of bread, yelping as they burned her fingers. "There must be something wrong with this thing. It's never done that before."

"You might like to remove the bacon as well," I said. "Zandra likes it crispy, but not cremated."

Vorana grabbed the spitting pan just in time. She opened a window to let the smoke out, waving her hands around. "I never burn bacon!"

Our three black kitten residents tumbled into the kitchen, play-fighting, a mass of fur and indignant hissing, their little tails in the air. A second later, Tempest and Wiggles showed up.

"Who burned the toast?" Tempest asked.

"The toaster," Vorana said. "I need a new one. Coffee's ready. Help yourself."

The kittens stalked over to Sage, but I warned them off with a hiss and a swipe of a paw. "She's not in the mood for playing. Or moving. Leave her alone."

Although the kittens tried to dodge around me and get to their snoozing target, I was having none of it. If Sage needed rest, then she'd get it. And as tempting as it was to eat her breakfast, I'd make sure Vorana saved her food.

I was worried about my curmudgeonly friend. She seemed out of sorts. When I had a moment to myself, I'd see if there was anything I could do to help.

Zandra was the last to amble into the kitchen. She wrinkled her nose at the smell of charring but said nothing as she joined Tempest at the table.

"The coffee is cold," Tempest muttered.

"It's not! I just made it," Vorana said. She reached for the coffeepot and touched the side. "How did that happen? I'm getting everything wrong this morning. Burnt toast. Over-crispy bacon. Now dodgy coffee. Are all my appliances going wrong?"

"I'm blaming the chef," Tempest whispered to Zandra.

Zandra shook her head before getting up to make fresh coffee.

When we'd returned home the previous evening, Tempest had appeared fine. She hadn't said much and wasn't interested in the investigation but had contentedly slouched around, listening to music and looking at her mobile snow globe. And the odd hackle lifting vibe had vanished. I was glad. She must have been having an off day. It happened with powerful magic. It got mean when it was twisted out of shape.

"I'm out of bread." Vorana appeared from the pantry. "I'm sure I had a fresh loaf. We could have bacon and blueberry muffins. And I've got fruit. Will that do for breakfast?"

"Sounds good to me," Zandra said.

"What are you doing today to make sure Tempest's name is cleared?" Wiggles sniffed around the kitchen floor for dropped food scraps.

"We found out from Erick's boss, Mr. Dimitri, that Erick had a difficult relationship with his family," I said. "We need to find out more about them and pay them a visit."

I'd told Wiggles about meeting Mr. Dimitri and discovering his tawdry love life and how we'd discounted him as a suspect. Although Finn was still checking Mr. Dimitri's and Lucinda's movements for the night of Erick's murder to ensure no more lies had snuck out.

"As long as I'm not charged with anything and I can get back to Willow Tree Falls soon, I don't care who did it." Tempest grabbed a blueberry muffin as soon as the plate was placed on the kitchen table.

"You don't care? We always help solve injustice," Wiggles said.

Tempest shrugged. "Maybe at home and when it involves demons, but this is different. This is a regular murder."

"There's nothing regular about murder." Vorana finally stopped fussing with the food and joined us at the table. "How's Randal dealing with all of this?" She addressed the question to Zandra.

Zandra didn't answer.

"He's sad," I said. "Randal was close with Erick. We should stop in and see how he's doing. Sorcha sent a food care parcel to cheer him up. One for you, too."

Zandra remained silent.

Tempest smirked. "Someone's in my sister's bad books."

"Randal should be in yours, too," Zandra said. "He thinks you're guilty of murder."

"Only because he panicked," I said. "He jumped to the wrong conclusion, and for that, he's genuinely sorry."

"Apology not accepted," Zandra said. "Let's change the subject."

We all ate and shuffled about in the tense atmosphere.

"What did you do yesterday that kept you so busy?" I asked Wiggles.

"Huh? What do you mean? We didn't do much. Slept a bunch. Ate. The usual."

"We sent several messages to see how things were going," I said.

"To me?" Wiggles shook his head. "I don't have a mobile snow globe."

"To Tempest and Vorana," I said. "Didn't you get them?"

Vorana looked puzzled. "I didn't get any messages. I was in the bookstore most of the day, but I came back here later to pick up a sweater. Nothing came through on my mobile. You sure you sent them to me?"

Zandra nodded. "Maybe there was a glitch, and they didn't get through."

"You don't need to check in on me," Tempest said. "We were fine. Once we got away from your grumpy angels, we just chilled. It's not like there's much to do around here."

"Crimson Cove is ten times the size of Willow Tree Falls," I said. "There's plenty to keep you occupied."

Vorana was looking at her mobile snow globe. "No messages. Something must have happened with the magic network." She stifled a yawn.

Sage howled and leapt into the air as the kittens set fire to her new prickly mat. "You irritating little furballs! Juno, obliterate them."

Everyone jumped up, and the fire was extinguished, but not before Sage's mat was charred beyond saving.

"Come here!" Tempest gathered up the kittens. "You're spending ten minutes on the naughty step because of that behavior. No more indoor fireballs. How many times do I have to tell you?"

The kittens meowed pitifully and lowered their ears.

"You're not winning me over with that pathetic act," Tempest said, though she was already smiling as she stroked them.

Wiggles puffed out smoke. "She never coos over me like that."

"It's because you're not an adorable bundle of kitten fluff. And they smell better than you," I muttered.

"She played with them for ages yesterday afternoon and ignored me, even when I exposed my belly and jiggled about on my back like a furry worm."

"Don't be jealous," I said. "You know what having youngsters is like. They want your full attention, or they misbehave."

"They destroy stuff that doesn't belong to them," Sage groused. "I just broke in that new door mat, and now look at it!"

"I'll get you another one," Vorana said. "Although perhaps I'll wait until the kittens have found new homes before putting anything flammable on the floor."

Sage huffed and grumbled while Vorana cleaned up the mess.

Tempest wandered off with the kittens in her arms, leaving Wiggles with a hangdog expression on his face.

"We'll figure out what's going on today," I said to him. "Then you can go back to Willow Tree Falls with Tempest, and you'll never have to see those kittens again."

"The sooner we escape from here, the better," he said. "I'm still worried about Tempest, though. I kept following her around yesterday until she snapped at me. She went out for a walk and didn't take me with her! That's wrong. I'm a hound. We walk!"

I patted his head with a velvet paw. "We'll make things right. You stay here and make sure she doesn't get into any trouble."

After Zandra helped the still-yawning Vorana take the remains of the prickly mat outside, we made our escape and headed to Angel Force to give Cythera an update.

When we arrived in the open-plan office, angels were bustling about, dashing in and out of the main door and fielding messages.

"Is there something going on in town we don't know about?" I asked Zandra. "A parade or market that's got everyone flustered?"

"Beats me. Maybe they're just pretending to be busy because Cythera shouted at them."

Finn waved us over. "How's it going?"

"It's been an eventful morning," I said. "It looks like the same for you."

"It's a strange morning. People keep showing up or leaving messages saying their magic keeps going wrong. At first, we thought it was just a few people trying spells beyond their abilities, but whatever it is, it's spreading."

"Is it something in the magic wards?" I asked. "If they're off-kilter, it'll affect magic users. It's happened before."

"I've messaged Randal to see if he can help," Finn said. "And I have an update about Dilbert Dimitri and Lucinda. The restaurant confirmed they dined together on the night of the murder. They're in the clear."

"You shouldn't be here." Cythera stamped over.

"Greetings! You're looking radiant as ever," I said.

She waved away my words. "Stay out of this investigation."

"That's not happening," Zandra said. "Not while you consider Tempest a suspect."

Cythera crossed her arms over her chest. "I had a formal complaint about you."

"About what, and who complained?" I asked.

"Mr. Dimitri is an influential figure in the business community," Cythera said. "He claims you've been stalking and harassing him."

"We were asking polite questions about Erick and their working relationship," I said. "Then we learned he'd been keeping secrets and mistreating Erick. Mr. Dimitri stole his ideas and sold them as his own."

"You have proof of that?"

"From a reliable source," I said. "Mr. Dimitri's secretary."

"Who had a crush on Erick," Zandra added. "She caught Mr. Dimitri snooping around Erick's desk and taking things."

Cythera's sharp expression suggested she didn't believe us. "Did you confront Mr. Dimitri in a restroom?"

"You're almost right," I said. "We checked his alibi for the evening of the murder. He said he was working late when Erick died, but his secretary said otherwise. And she was right. Mr. Dimitri has a mistress, and he's been spending a lot of time with her. That's who we confronted in the restroom."

"You admit to harassment?" Cythera asked.

"Mr. Dimitri looked guilty," Zandra snapped.

"Tempest looks much guiltier to me!"

Zandra took a step toward Cythera. "Stop focusing on Tempest. If you do, you'll make a mistake you may not come back from."

"Is that a threat?" Cythera squared off with Zandra. "My angels heard that. I should arrest you."

"What for? Doing your job?" I jumped onto Zandra's shoulder in an attempt to defuse the tension. "No threats were issued."

"Tempest had better be behaving," Cythera said, after eyeballing Zandra for several silent seconds.

"She's been as good as gold," I replied.

"She was seen lurking around town yesterday."

"There was no lurking. Tempest was most likely taking an innocent walk."

Cythera's eyes narrowed. "I don't trust her. Tell her to stay at home and out of people's way."

"Tempest isn't a prisoner!" Zandra said. "And she needs to take Wiggles for a walk."

"He walks himself," Cythera said. "He walked right in here yesterday and stole three lunches from the fridge. Tell him to stay at home, too. They're menaces."

"They're currently at Vorana's, enjoying breakfast," I said.

Cythera grunted, showing her displeasure. "This is your final warning. If you keep harassing people in an attempt to get a confession to save Tempest, you'll find yourself in the same trouble as your demon hunting sister."

I sent a wave of calm over Zandra as magic sparked off her fingers. "Not now. We have a bigger fight to deal with."

She sighed, pressing her fingertips against her forehead. "Cythera, you'd be just like me if an innocent family member was accused of murder."

"I'd remain professional. I always do. Leave this alone." Cythera turned and stomped back to her office.

"I know you won't do that," Finn said after Cythera had slammed her door. "Is there anything I can do to help?"

"When we met Mr. Dimitri yesterday, he mentioned Erick's family," I said.

"Such as it is," Finn replied.

"What do you know about them?"

"The only immediate family left are his sister and a brother—Jazzi and Langdon."

"Do they live nearby?" Zandra asked.

Finn wrote down their details. "Go carefully with this one. Cythera has been even spikier than usual. She'll lock you up if you test her patience. She's yelled at everyone this morning."

"Perhaps she argued with Maverick," I said. "Maybe he made her breakfast wrong, and she got mad. Vorana burned the toast and the bacon this morning, so we didn't have the best start, either."

"Burned bacon. What a waste. Ask your questions but keep it on the down-low. Cythera was spitting mad when Mr. Dimitri's complaint came in. Apparently, he donates to the Angel Force Charitable Fund. He was hinting whether he'd do it this year since he'd been so unfairly treated by untrained investigators."

"Untrained! As you know, we're the best you've got," I said.

Finn chuckled. "You won't hear me dispute that."

"Come with us," I said. "That way, we can make it official. And I've missed spending time with you. You've been away from Crimson Cove for too long."

Finn looked at the pile of messages on his desk. "I could do with a break from this chaos."

I gestured at the door. "Let's escape before Cythera starts yelling again."

Chapter 14

Ties that bind

We used Zandra's van to make the forty-minute drive to Badger's Haze. Although the village name was cute, the area had a reputation for trouble. As we cruised along the main street, it was clear little love was given to this sad place. Many of the houses were boarded up or in desperate need of repair. The streets were grimy, and every window box held only long-expired ghosts of plants, jutting out like spectral fingers.

Finn whistled low as we drove past a burned-down house. "I've heard about Badger's Haze, but I've never visited. It's as bad as everyone says."

"I've heard rumors it's cursed," Zandra said. "Sorcha told me about it. Something to do with a coven of witches that got themselves in deep using the wrong magic. They were trying to regenerate the village and covered it with a spell that backfired. Every good deed is flipped on its head."

"Would that mean every bad deed would become a good deed?" I asked. "Maybe the magic works in reverse."

"Let's not linger here too long to find out," Finn said. "My background check on Erick's family revealed they have their troubles, too."

"With Angel Force?" I asked.

"Nothing serious. Erick's late father got in trouble for small-time stealing. His older brother, Langdon, has been caught with illegal magic a few times."

"What kind of spells are we talking about?" Zandra turned off the main road, heading toward our destination, having to steer around holes to avoid wheel damage.

"Nothing that would harm anyone," Finn said, "but he uses potions and combinations of herbs to heighten his senses."

"Drugs," I said. "Magically infused drugs. He uses?"

"Langdon served a short stretch in jail because he got caught with too much on him, and there was concern he was dealing," Finn said. "He promised he wasn't, but he knew the rules and broke them."

"What about the sister?" I asked.

"Jazzi has no criminal past," Finn said. "We couldn't find much about her. She skims below the radar."

"Maybe she's the family's criminal mastermind," I said. "Jazzi keeps a low profile because she's up to no good."

"We'll soon find out. This is the house." Zandra pulled up outside a single-story detached home. There was a chain-link fence around a neglected patch of brown grass. Some of the wooden siding on the house had fallen off, exposing rotten wood. There was a single garage next to the house and an old, rusted red car in front of it.

"Have they been told what happened to Erick?" I hopped off Finn's lap and stretched so he could get out of the van.

"They know."

"How did they take the news?"

"It was hard to tell. I spoke to Jazzi. She sighed a few times, grumbled about having to arrange a funeral, and then hung up before I could say much else."

"Mr. Dimitri said the relationship between Erick and his family was poor." Zandra pocketed her keys then headed to the rusted, open gate.

"The way Jazzi spoke, it seemed like they had no relationship," Finn said.

The front door opened. A tall, bony woman with startling blonde hair and a scowl on her face stepped out. She wore a rainbow-colored dressing gown and slippers on her feet. "What do you want?"

Finn introduced us all.

"You still haven't told me what you want." Jazzi jammed her hands on her hips. "If you're here about Erick, I already know. Erick's friend called about it. And then someone from Angel Force contacted me."

"That was me," Finn said.

"We're sorry for your loss," I said.

"Don't be. I didn't like Erick. We had nothing in common."

"Even so, he was your brother," I said.

"I didn't ask him to be my brother. If there's something I need to sign or you have his things, I'll take those. But that's it."

"Could we come in?" Finn asked.

"No. I'm busy."

"Getting ready for work?" I asked.

Jazzi pursed her lips. "I'm not working at the moment. I'm still busy, though."

Finn glanced at us. "As you know, we're investigating what happened to Erick."

"Randal said someone knocked him down with a spell. He probably tripped over his own feet trying to get away. Erick was clumsy. If he wasn't leering at a woman's chest, he was in his own head, rather than the real world. He made a ton of money, but all that's done is get him killed. Better to be poor, then no one bothers you."

"Do you think someone killed Erick for his money?" I asked.

"I couldn't tell you. But when you get things, people always want to take them from you."

"The last time you spoke to Erick, was he concerned about anyone bothering him or asking for money?" Finn asked.

"I can't remember the last time we spoke. Erick was a stranger to me. As soon as he got lucky and landed his first job, he abandoned us. I thought family was supposed to look out for each other."

"How did you look out for Erick?" I asked.

Jazzi's nostrils flared. "I did when we were kids, but he made it hard. He had terrible allergies and a permanently dripping nose. So gross. And he'd always leer at girls way out of his league. Including my friends! He was a creeper."

"Did you spend much time together when you were younger?"

"We liked different things. He was into all that dumb fantasy stuff. Dragons and dungeons. Why would I want anything to do with that?"

"You must have been happy for Erick when he made a name for himself with his tech magic," I said.

Jazzi sniffed. "I would have been, if he'd bothered to remember who I was." She sounded jealous of Erick's success.

"Did you ever ask him for help?" I asked.

"What do I need help with? I have everything I need right here. My palace. A car. No worries."

I glanced at the sad little house. Maybe Jazzi was being truthful. Some people were fine with living a simpler life.

"Erick was always showing off, going on about some new game he invented or some tedious gadget that was supposed to change the world. I lost interest. We had nothing in common other than the same parents and that we were dragged up in this place."

"Where were you when you heard about Erick's murder?" Zandra asked.

"Why do you care?"

Finn gently cleared his throat. "When a murder occurs, we always speak to those closest to the victim. Just to rule them out."

Jazzi jabbed a finger against her chest. "Me! You think I had anything to do with this?"

"As Finn said, it's just to rule you out," I said.

Her expression turned smug. "I was on a hot date. I'll give you the guy's information. And I wouldn't waste my time doing anything bad to Erick. What would it get me if I did?"

Finn took a note of the details of the man Jazzi had gone on a date with. "Thank you. You can't think of anyone who had a problem with Erick?"

Jazzi's gaze flicked to the garage. "Talk to Langdon, my other useless brother. The idiot probably killed him for a dare."

"A dare!" Zandra said. "Why would he do that?"

"Because he has no brain in that enormous head of his, and he does things because he thinks they're funny. Everything's a joke to Langdon. But he's the biggest joke of all. He's almost forty and a squatter."

"A squatter? Does Langdon not live with you?" Finn asked.

"I kicked him out of the house, but he refuses to leave," Jazzi said. "So, I make him sleep in the garage."

I stared at the small garage next to the house. "You own this home together?"

Jazzi nodded. "When Dad died, he left the house to all of us. I was renting a place nearby, and so was Langdon, but we both moved back here to save money."

"What did Erick do with his share of the house?" Finn asked.

"He didn't need this place. Did you know Erick had three houses? He never let any of us stay in them. What's one guy need three houses for? He always was selfish."

"Erick let you stay here even though he owned a third of the property?" I asked.

"He oh-so-generously gifted his share to us," Jazzi said. "We did it legally. We had to pay him a token amount—something to do with taxes and legal jargon. I didn't understand it. He got the payment, and we got his share of this place."

"That sounds generous," I said. "Erick could have kept his share or insisted you sell the house to release the funds."

"I deserved this house," Jazzi said. "Erick abandoned us for a nerd career. And I know he was ashamed of us. He never invited me over to his place, and he barely called. He got a lucky break and left us behind."

"Why did you kick Langdon out of the house?" Finn asked.

"He set fire to the kitchen while making French fries. The loser fell asleep in a chair. I told him not to use the stove when he was doped up, but he didn't listen. He's lucky I didn't have him arrested for damaging my place."

"We'd like to speak to him," Finn said.

"Good luck with that. He rarely gets up before noon." Jazzi pointed at the garage. "Just hammer on it until he answers." She stepped back inside the house and shut the door.

"There's little love there for Erick," I said as we headed toward the garage.

"Active hatred, I'd say," Zandra replied. "Jazzi is jealous of Erick's success. The way she talked, it sounds as if she expected a handout because he'd become the successful sibling."

"Perhaps Erick didn't visit or call as often as he should," I said, "but with a welcome like that, who could blame him?"

Finn knocked on the metal garage door several times. It reverberated under his hand, but no one called out to say they were coming.

He had to knock for several minutes before there were shuffling and scraping sounds from the other side. A few seconds later, the garage door slowly squeaked up on poorly oiled hinges. A tall, gangly man with messy, dirty blond hair, wearing only a pair of jogging bottoms, slowly revealed himself.

"Langdon Farten?" Finn asked.

Langdon blinked at us, looking like a startled bat that had fallen out of his tree. "I was the last time I checked. Why you bangin' on my pad at this early hour?"

"It's not that early," I said and did a swift round of introductions.

Langdon nodded slowly as he scratched at the hair on his chest. "You here about Erick?"

"We'd like to talk to you if you've got a few minutes," Finn said.

Langdon fumbled around in his pockets before pulling out a pair of sunglasses and sliding them into place. "Sure. Come in. Excuse the mess. I had a party last night. Does anyone want coffee? If you do, get me one. Extra strong. Lots of sugar."

"We're good, thanks," Zandra said. "Were you celebrating something last night?"

Langdon shuffled back to the single bed wedged in one corner of the room and sat on the edge. There was only one fold-out chair, so we remained standing. "Nothing special. I just had friends over. It got rowdy."

"Did Jazzi join you?" I asked.

Langdon chuckled then winced and pressed his fingers to his forehead. "She doesn't know what the word party means. She's way too uptight to have fun. She yelled at us to keep the noise down and threatened to call Angel Force if we didn't shut up."

"Did Erick ever come to your parties?" I asked.

"Erick? No, we didn't have that kind of bro thing happening." Langdon lifted a pack of beers from beside his bed. He cracked one open. "Does anyone else want one?"

"Not for us," Zandra said. "You weren't close to Erick?"

"I wasn't in his life, not really," Langdon said. "We hung out together when we were younger, but he was into nerdy stuff, while I liked partying and sports. We ignored each other as we got older. It wasn't anything bad, just one of those things. I was surprised what happened to him. He wasn't a guy who took risks. Most people didn't notice him."

"What did you think of his success?" I asked.

Langdon downed some of his beer. "Erick was smart. He always saw a big future, whereas I only ever saw this." He gestured around his home. "This is perfect for today, and that's all I focus on. After all, who knows what's coming your way? Erick wouldn't have known this was coming for him. He worked hard, never did anything fun. That's a waste of a life. Do you play?"

"Play what?" Finn asked.

"Online! Games. You know. Shoot 'em ups." Langdon rolled off the bed and sat on a large cushion on the floor in front of a big TV. "This is one of Erick's. I like his games. He stopped doing design and moved into apps and products, though. Not fun."

"I'll try." I walked over and jabbed a paw on the control several times.

"Little dude, you may need thumbs for this."

"I'm a dudette. And you could be right." I jabbed some more and achieved nothing but a chuckle from Langdon.

"When was the last time you spoke to your brother?" Finn asked.

"It's been a while."

"Is there anyone you can think of who'd want to harm him?" Finn said.

"No, but like I said, we ran with different crowds." Langdon set aside the controller and jumped to his feet. "Man, I'm starved. I always get the munchies after a party." He walked to the door and grabbed his jacket.

Underneath the jacket was a dartboard. Erick's face was on it.

Chapter 15

Darted dude

"You use Erick's picture for target practice?" I asked. The dartboard image had three darts sticking out of it and had clearly been well used, since it was covered in pin holes.

"Oh! That. I'd forgotten it was there." Langdon shrugged on his jacket. "How about we deal with these munchies?"

"How about you tell us why your dead brother's face is an acceptable target for your darts?" Finn asked.

"It's not! Like I said, it's no big deal. I could go for tacos. Who wants tacos?" Langdon asked.

"No food until you tell the truth," I said.

Langdon pressed a hand to his stomach. "I have low blood sugar. I'll faint if I don't eat."

Zandra glowered at him. "Did you put Erick's face on that dartboard?"

"Maybe. I forget. We could go for pastries. There's nothing good to eat around here, but if you have wheels, I know a place."

"Stop thinking about your stomach," I said.

"It's grumbling. It won't let me think about anything else."

"Did Erick know his face was on your dartboard?" I asked.

"Sure. He stopped by all the time, and we'd play together. It was a joke."

"How is it possible you played together if you'd lost touch?" Finn asked.

"I... well, he came by now and again. Not so much lately. We played then. He was the one who suggested putting his face on that board."

"Why would Erick do that?" Zandra asked.

"For jokes!"

"You said your brother was work focused and no fun. Which version of Erick are we supposed to believe in?" I asked.

"Can't a dude be both?"

"Not according to you," I said. "You said Erick wasted his life by investing in his career. If that's true, then Erick doesn't seem like the kind of person to think throwing darts at an image of himself would be entertaining."

"Maybe... um... maybe it wasn't him who put his face on the board. It could have been someone else," Langdon said.

"Who?" Zandra asked. "You said you didn't know if Erick had enemies. Were you lying about that, too?"

"No! No lies. I'm a straight-up guy. I live in the moment. No point dwelling on the past or focusing on a future that's yet to exist."

"If you don't focus on your future, you end up living in your sister's garage after she kicked you out of the house," I said. "And forethought, when you cook your French fries, is always sensible. It avoids houses burning to the ground."

"But you never know what'll happen from moment to moment," Langdon said. "We could go for sausage patties for breakfast. I know a great café. Well, roadside place on wheels. It's clean, though. No rodents."

Finn sighed. "Tell us the truth about Erick. When was the last time you really saw him?"

"I… I don't know. I can't think when I'm this hungry. Take me for breakfast. That'll help. It'll all make sense then."

"You've made little sense since we started talking to you," I said.

"Let me grab my beer. I think clearer when I'm drinking."

I exchanged an irritated glance with Zandra. Langdon seemed almost too dumb to be a killer. Or was this an act? He was deflecting in the hope we'd get tired and abandon our questioning.

Langdon jogged over to his bed and grabbed his half-drunk beer. He took a swig. "That's better. I'm still hungry, though."

"Get something from the kitchen," I said.

"Jazzi doesn't let me in the house when she's home. She says I stink the place out. She's so mean."

"You have no food here?"

"Only in the trash. Chips and dip from last night's partying. I could take a look and see if anything could be saved. Do you want anything?"

"No! No eating the trash," I said.

Langdon stood there, beer in hand and jogging pants hanging dangerously low on his hips. His expression turned desperate. "What do you want me to say?"

"Tell us the truth," Finn said. "You must have had a problem with Erick if you're throwing darts at his face."

"It was nothing serious. Erick could be like Jazzi. He'd get uptight and serious and talk about things I didn't understand. He barely drank, too. What kind of person doesn't drink?"

"Someone who wants a clear head and not to be hung over every morning," I said.

"Erick said beer impaired his magic, whatever that means," Langdon said.

"Do you have tech mage magic, too?" Zandra asked.

"It skipped me. I can do a few basic spells, but nothing like Erick."

"You were jealous of his abilities?" I asked.

"No! He did what made him happy, and I do what makes me happy. It's a win-win."

"Not for Erick, since he's dead," I said. "Do you know when your brother died?"

"Sure. At least, I think Jazzie said. I was sleeping when she yelled the news at me."

"What did you do that night?"

"Hung out here with buddies. Same as most nights. It's good to party."

"Talk us through this party," I said. "Did you leave at any point?"

"Hold up. This is getting serious, and I don't do well with serious." Langdon set down his beer and finally pulled up his jogging pants. "I know my limits. I'm not smart like Erick. I wouldn't have the first idea how to kill someone. And I know I'd never get away with it, so why bother trying?"

"You tried lying to us," Finn said. "You didn't like your own brother. What did Erick do that was so bad you had to kill him?"

"Nothing! I don't like where this is going." Langdon inched toward the garage door. "I wanted Erick to be more like me. Hang out and enjoy life. I begged him to make more games. He said the big money was in products for non-magicals. How boring is that?"

"Were you envious of his success at work?" Zandra asked.

"Envy is a pointless emotion," Langdon said. "I read that on the side of a milk carton. Or was it the side of a bus? I forget."

"Wise words," I said. "Many people feel envy, and some of them act on it."

"Not me. I was partying with my friends the night Erick died. We partied hard, Jazzi yelled at us as usual, and I passed out. That was it. I don't even know where Erick lives, so how would I know where to find him to hurt him?"

"He was killed in Crimson Cove," Finn said. "Didn't Jazzi tell you that?"

"Huh! Yeah, I think so. A cove. Like on a beach?"

"We have a beach," Finn said. "Erick was killed by a powerful spell."

"Then it definitely wasn't me."

"He looked scared when he died," I said. "Someone wanted him terrified as he took his last breath."

Langdon ran a hand over his pale stubble. "I wouldn't want to do that to my brother. We weren't close, but being scared sucks. I really need to eat."

"You really need to come with me," Finn said.

"Why? You can't charge me! I did nothing."

"You need to answer more questions," Finn said. "And I need to check your alibi for the night of Erick's murder. Give me a list of the friends who came to this party."

"They hate angels. No offense, man, but they'll be unnerved. I don't want my friends being messed with."

"Let us mess with them, or you'll be stuck in a cell until we get the truth out of you," I said.

"Nope. No cell for me. I don't do well in tiny spaces." Langdon pressed a hand on a button on the wall, and the garage door creaked up.

"Don't even think about leaving," Finn said.

"I've got to eat!"

"You've got to answer my questions."

The garage door opened painfully slowly, so there was no risk of Langdon escaping. It creaked and complained, threatening to stop moving at any second. Finn approached Langdon, making sure he couldn't bolt for the exit once the gap was big enough to get out of.

"Relax. I really do just need to find food," Langdon said. "I promise I'll take you to the best place. If you buy me breakfast, I'll tell you everything."

"Including your confession to murder?" I asked.

"I didn't kill Erick! I don't lie."

"You weren't telling the whole truth about how you felt about Erick, though," I said.

"I... remind me what I said again?" Langdon stepped outside.

Jazzi appeared and whacked him on the side of the head with a lump of wood.

Langdon yelped and staggered, falling to his knees. "What did you do that for?"

Jazzi brandished the wood over Langdon. "I was listening, and you've been lying to this angel. You did it, didn't you? You stinking, cheating, halfwit of a moron. You killed Erick!"

"My head! It's bleeding." Langdon held a hand against his head.

Jazzi raised the wood again, but Finn stepped in front of her. "I'd advise against doing that. Langdon could have you arrested for assault. We saw everything."

"He killed Erick! I could be next. He's unhinged. Get him off the streets and away from me."

"You're the unhinged one. My head really hurts!" Langdon stayed down, still holding his head.

"Langdon has always been jealous and immature," Jazzi said. "He never thinks through his actions. My kitchen still smells of smoke and oil because he didn't know how to make his own fries. He's a waste of space. Put him away. It's the best place for him."

"I feel sick," Langdon said.

"Let's go into the house," I said. "I'll check your head injury, and we can talk without the neighbors watching."

Jazzi twisted around and waved a fist at several houses. "Such a bunch of nosy losers around here. We'll be the talk of the town, thanks to you."

"You hit me! The neighbors all know you're unstable. They'll gossip about you." Langdon whined as Zandra helped him to his feet.

"I don't want you here," Jazzi yelled. "Get your junk from the garage and leave."

"I own half this house! I only moved into the garage because I couldn't stand your sniping and all those stinky candles you're always lighting."

"And I can't stand your stench. The greasy food and those gross socks you leave lying everywhere," Jazzi said.

"I hate your face. Change it."

"Change your attitude. And when did you last wash those joggers?"

"I really think we should take this inside," I said. "Langdon's head wound is bleeding badly."

Jazzi tossed aside the wood, turned, and stomped away.

"That's as good of an invitation as we're getting." Finn turned to Langdon. "Are you okay to walk?"

"Are there two of you? Am I seeing double?" Langdon asked.

"He could have a concussion," Zandra said.

It took a few minutes and a very wobbly Langdon, but we finally got into the house. It was cold and dreary. The rooms were small and dark, and Jazzi refused to put on overhead lights, saying they were too expensive to run. Instead, she lit several smoking candles and set them on the small kitchen table. She wouldn't let us into the living room.

She wrinkled her nose as Finn helped Langdon sit in a chair. "Don't get blood on my floor. It'll never come out."

"I'll put blood on the floor if I want to, since it's my floor, too." Langdon leaned forward, trying to get blood to drip off his chin.

"Stop him! I never come into your garage and mess about," Jazzi said. "That's your space. This is mine."

"I come in here all the time." Langdon winced as I inspected his wound. "I use your shower stuff, too. I like the shampoo. It smells of lemons. I use it everywhere. Get it in all the crevices. It tingles."

"You're disgusting," Jazzi said. "I wish you were dead and not Erick. At least he left me alone."

"And I wish you had a sense of humor and knew how to smile," Langdon said.

"That's enough!" Finn said. "Juno, how's the head looking?"

"It'll be sore, even after it's healed. Do you have any objections if I cast a spell over you?"

"Will it make me puke?" Langdon asked.

"No, you should feel better."

"Any weird side effects? Extra limbs? Lose my interest in alcohol? Feel the need to get a job?"

"None of those side effects are real," I said. "Of course, if you want to go to the local doctor—"

"We don't have one," Jazzi said. "The last guy was chased out. Nobody likes a know-it-all."

"Surely, you'd prefer a know-it-all doctor to an incompetent, know nothing doctor," I said.

"He was too smug. He looked down his nose at us," Jazzi said. "He left, and no one took his place."

181

"Then let's get you fixed up the best we can, and then we'll talk," I said.

Jazzi grudgingly got us glasses of tepid water from the faucet while I healed Langdon.

His stomach gurgled as I removed my paw from his head. "Thanks, little dudette. I do feel better. Still hungry, though."

"I'm not feeding you," Jazzi said. "You stole that lump of cheese from the fridge. I'm changing the locks."

"Let's focus on Erick," Finn said to Jazzi. "Do you really think Langdon killed him?"

"If she's blaming me, then I'm blaming her," Langdon said. "She hated Erick. She was crazy jealous of his success. She'd complain that he never sent her money, and he was living the high life while making fun of us."

"He could have sent us some money," Jazzi said. "We're hardly living the life of luxury."

"You've got the house. I've got my garage," Langdon said. "That's a treat. Some people have nowhere to live."

"In case you hadn't noticed, this place is falling apart." Jazzi glared at a hanging cabinet door. "Neither of us has the funds to fix anything."

Zandra flicked the light switch. Nothing happened. "No power?"

"We got cut off a couple of months ago," Jazzi said. "It's a mistake. The dumb company said we owe them money, and until we pay, we won't have any power. No one listens to me when I tell them we've paid and they're the ones in the wrong."

There was a loud rap on the front door.

"Who's pestering us now?" Jazzi stomped off to answer it. There were a few seconds of silence then a thump and a squeak.

A broad-shouldered, grey-skinned man with pale blue eyes appeared in the kitchen doorway. "Good day, folks. I won't be long. I'm here to collect my dues."

"Dues? What's he talking about?" Langdon asked.

"I sent several warning notices that I'd be visiting," the man said. "I'm from Bluff and Bailey's Removal Company."

"Removals? Are you a bailiff?" Finn asked.

"The paperwork is all here." The man handed it over to Finn. "I need to seize assets in the amount of the debt owed." He looked around the kitchen and frowned. "Although you may not have enough for me to take. Where do you keep your valuables?"

Finn read through the letter he'd been handed. "It's legit."

Jazzi appeared in the doorway. "I told him we have nothing. He's another one who won't listen."

"And as I explained in my letters and the messages you never replied to, you have a substantial debt owed to several companies," the bailiff said. "They've been generous with their terms and have given you more time. You must repay what you owe."

"With what?" Jazzi flapped her arms around. "I've got nothing."

The bailiff sighed. "And as that letter outlines, if you're unable to pay the debt owed, you forfeit this house and the contents."

"We can't!" Langdon staggered to his feet. "Where will we live?"

"Did Erick know about your financial difficulties?" I asked.

"I may have mentioned it," Jazzi said. "Not that he cared."

"Did you ask him for some money, and he refused to help?"

"I shouldn't have needed to ask," Jazzi said. "Erick was loaded. You know about the three houses already. He spent so much on useless games and gadgets."

"Where shall I start?" the bailiff asked.

"Give us a minute," Finn said. "There's been a death in the family."

"I'm sorry to hear that." The bailiff hesitated. "I'll take a look around. Let me know when you're ready." He left the kitchen.

"Will Erick's death buy us more time to pay the debts?" There was a whining note in Jazzi's voice. "They could take pity on us if they think we're grieving."

"Is that all you care about?" Langdon asked.

"Someone has to care!" Jazzi scuttled closer to Finn. "If Langdon is a killer, will the debt company leave me alone? I could say he bullied me into taking on all the debt and stopped me from paying the bills because he spent it all on beer. Would that work?"

"Hey! You're pointing the finger at me, but you were the one who always complained about Erick," Langdon said.

"You did, too. You're as bad as me," Jazzi said. "You act all bro this and fun times that, but you're stressed and miserable. That's why you're always off your gourd. It's got nothing to do with you living in the moment. You just don't face it because it's so grim."

"Have you told this angel you've been speaking to Erick behind my back?" Langdon scowled at Jazzi.

"Liar!" she screeched.

"I overheard a conversation you had on the globe. You were angry with him. So angry that maybe you killed him."

Jazzi tried to shove Langdon, but Finn stepped between them.

"Stay out of my business!" Jazzi hissed. "I couldn't have killed Erick because I was on a date. You know I was."

"Date? Hah! Don't make me laugh. That date was a miserable failure. You tried to sneak back here, but I saw you come home early." Langdon sneered at Jazzi.

"I did not! I went on a date with a hot guy. I've already told this angel that."

"The hot guy who ditched you before dessert and left you to pay the bill," Langdon said with a smirk.

Jazzi bared her discolored teeth at him. "You could easily have killed Erick and forgotten about it. You've messed up your head with all those weird herbs you snort."

"You got dumped before dessert, so you took it out on Erick. Poor guy. Erick probably tried to comfort you, and you took offense."

"It was you. You said you were at your dumb party with your even dumber friends, but I checked on you before I went to bed. Your friends were passed out, and you were nowhere to be seen. Off killing Erick, were you?"

Langdon froze in his seat. "I must have been out the back, having a smoke."

"Enough blame shifting," Finn said. "You're hiding things, and I don't trust your alibis. You're both coming to Angel Force until I learn more."

As Jazzi and Langdon protested, I had to agree with Finn. Erick's siblings were troubled. Perhaps troubled enough to be involved in this murder.

Chapter 16

Sibling rivalry

Rather than taking the squabbling siblings to Crimson Cove in Zandra's van, which would have been a squeeze and resulted in Zandra blasting them with a spell, I magicked Jazzi and Langdon to Crimson Cove. Zandra and Finn drove back in the van.

When we arrived at Angel Force, things were different. The hectic buzz had gone, and no angels dashed around, fielding messages and calls.

"Wait here," I said to Jazzi and Langdon and gestured for them to take a seat. "I need to find an angel to process you."

"We're not going in a cell," Jazzi said. "We've done nothing wrong. Well, at least I haven't. You can put this loser in isolation and toss the key down a drain for all I care."

"I've got nothing to hide," Langdon said. "It was you."

"Pipe down," Jazzi snapped. "You're under the influence from everything you sniffed, ate, or drank last night. Angel Force won't believe a word you say."

"They'll believe me when I say you have a black heart and a vicious tongue. And you look like a unicorn stamped on your face."

I left them squabbling and nudged open Cythera's office door with my head. She was bent over official-looking paperwork, a scowl on her face.

"Greetings! I bring you two suspects in Erick's murder. His brother and sister."

"Why are you the one bringing them in?" Cythera didn't look up from her paperwork. "I know Finn snuck off with you when he was supposed to be fielding calls. Where is he?"

"Finn and Zandra aren't far behind me," I said. "What's that you're looking at?"

"Angel Force business that has nothing to do with you." She slapped a hand on the paperwork. "Why are you bothering me?"

"Someone needs to deal with the suspects, and you're the only angel in the building. And as advanced as my intellect is, I've never taken the time to learn your procedures for booking in suspects for questioning."

Cythera shoved back her seat and shook out her wings. "Why do you think they're involved?"

"Langdon and Jazzi are claiming each other did it," I said. "And there's no affection for Erick."

"Motive?"

"They have debt problems, and Erick didn't help them get out of their financial mess. I have a feeling it's a mess of their own making, but they expected him to fix it for them because he made himself a fortune."

"How true is your story?" Cythera remained standing behind her desk, not looking impressed by my superb deduction skills.

"I'm offended you doubt my word. But I have witnesses. Zandra and Finn were there when Jazzi and Langdon revealed their true colors. It wasn't pretty. Voices were raised. Fingers jabbed. All dramatic and unnecessary. If you poke your head out of the door, you'll hear it still going on."

"You'd do anything to ensure Tempest seems innocent," Cythera said. "She's your witch's sister, so you're duty-bound to protect her."

"Untrue. If Wiggles was saying all of this, I'd expect your doubt to shine through like a ray of sunshine. But you know me. We've worked together for so long now we're practically family. Close, supportive, wonderful family."

Cythera grunted. "We are nowhere near family. Although there are certain family members I do my best to avoid."

"Find yourself a shot of optimism, or this day will only get worse," I said. "If you still have Tempest as your prime suspect, then you're bound to look in the wrong place. And you know what that means."

"A successful conviction because I'm never wrong."

"More paperwork."

"I have no issue with paperwork. I'm focused on the trouble, and it keeps coming back to Tempest and that dreadful creature she takes with her everywhere."

"What's Wiggles done wrong?" I asked.

"He's causing chaos. Residents keep seeing him around town, followed by three black kittens. They're often running after him to keep up with his misbehavior."

"Those kittens are staying with Vorana until we find them permanent homes," I said. "They like Tempest, but they're not keen on Wiggles."

"He's leading them into trouble," Cythera said. "They all appear just before problems start. That's where my angels are. Fixing that hellhound's mischief! Tempest must be making him cause distractions to buy herself more time before the inevitable happens."

"That makes no sense. Wiggles is too worried about Tempest to mess around," I said. "He has a cheeky side, but only when he's not occupied with ensuring his extremely innocent witch isn't tried for a crime she had nothing to do with."

"So why is he always seen just before chaos breaks out?"

"It could be a coincidence," I said.

"You don't believe in those."

"Wiggles could be helping prevent a worse trouble from happening," I said. "You're always so quick to think the worst of people."

"With good reason. The people I deal with are criminals. Low-lives. Annoyances."

"Wiggles has never gotten himself in trouble," I said.

"We both know that's untrue. I intend to ask him what he's doing and who ordered him to do it," Cythera said.

"Add that task to the bottom of your list," I said. "As of this moment, you have two ideal suspects in Erick's murder waiting in the office."

Cythera peered out the door and sighed. "I'll speak to them."

"Wait for Finn to get back. You're pricklier than usual, and you don't want them to clam up and refuse to speak when you do that intimidating wing fluttering and grousing."

"You're telling me how to do my job?" Cythera flared her wings. "Are you sure that's sensible?"

"Given the mood you're in, I'd say no," I said. "Not had enough caffeine today?"

"Leave. You're annoying me."

"Before I do, how's Charlie? The last time I checked, there was no update from the hospital."

"As far as I know, the situation is the same." Cythera made a shooing gesture.

"And the results from the tests on Erick's body?"

"Unhelpful."

"You found nothing to pinpoint what killed Erick and knocked Charlie out?"

"Magic! Something dark. That's as good as it gets."

"Shall I take a look at Erick?"

"Are you suggesting we made an error?" Her icy blue gaze sparked with rage.

"The thought never crossed my mind. This lack of evidence means Jazzi and Langdon must be interrogated as a matter of urgency," I said. "If they tell you the spell used, we can reverse the aftereffects and save Charlie."

"If it was them who cast the spell," Cythera said. "Have you bothered to test their magic to see how powerful they are?"

I hesitated. If Langdon had told the truth, he had no advanced magic. Jazzi seemed equally down on her luck when it came to powers, but maybe she was lazy and didn't practice. She didn't strike me as a hyper-motivated person.

Cythera sighed. "Leave it to me, as usual. But if I find you've wasted my time—"

"I'll ensure our suspects are settled, and when Finn and Zandra get here, you question them."

"Thank you so much for my orders."

"You're welcome. It always pays to be efficient."

Thirty minutes passed, and in that time, Cythera didn't leave her office once. That meant I had to entertain Jazzi and Langdon, who continued to snipe at each other and accuse the other of murder. It was a relief when Finn and Zandra finally showed up.

"How's everything going?" Finn appeared in the kitchen doorway with Zandra, where I'd been sitting, listening to the unpleasantly sharp sibling banter being tossed around the room like spiky, gassy enchanted hedgehogs.

"Things are tense," I said. "Cythera said you were in charge of the interviews."

Finn glanced at Cythera's closed door. "She's still having a bad day?"

"She must have rolled out of bed on the wrong side, stepped on a plug, and run out of coffee," I said. "And I suspect there was no hot water when she took a shower. I imagine Maverick enjoys a long

192

morning groom. His mane of hair must need regular maintenance."

Finn failed to suppress a chuckle. "You two, with me. I'll get you processed."

"Processed for what?" Jazzi asked.

"Processed to spend the rest of your life behind bars," Langdon said. "There's no doubt it was you."

"Why wasn't it you? Maybe your two brain cells smashed together and gave you a dumb idea to kill Erick."

"Let's not start that again." Finn gestured for Jazzi and Langdon to leave the kitchen. "Thanks, Juno. I'll take it from here."

I hopped onto Zandra's shoulder as he led the protesting siblings out of the kitchen and settled them in separate interview rooms.

"We should check in with Barney, or he'll think we've left Crimson Cove for good," Zandra said.

"We need to do something before that," I said. "Cythera said there's no update about Charlie. We should visit the hospital and see how he's doing."

"We could, but they don't like you being there," Zandra said.

"Foolish regulations about hygiene and fur. I'm a magical cat! You go in, and I'll sneak through a window. If Charlie is awake, he can tell us what happened. That'll clear Tempest's name, and maybe settle the finger of blame firmly on Langdon or Jazzi."

"Or both of them. Let me drop Barney a message, so he knows we haven't forgotten him." Zandra was already tapping on her mobile snow globe. "And

I'll message Tempest, too, and make sure she's not bored."

"Get her to warn Wiggles to behave. He's been seen out with the kittens. They've been getting into trouble." I leaned against Zandra's head as I waited for her to send the messages.

"Got it. Let's go," she said.

We got back in the van, and I was happy to settle into the soft, comfortable bed on the passenger seat. It needed to be moved to make room for Finn, and I had no objection, since he was a good friend, but it was a much more comfortable ride snuggled in softness.

"Cythera said something that made me doubt Langdon and Jazzi's guilt," I said.

"Go on." Zandra navigated through the traffic, heading toward the small hospital.

"The magic used to kill Erick was extraordinary," I said. "When we got to Randal's house, the atmosphere was unpleasantly electric. Serious power had flooded through the building. Dark power. I didn't feel that on Langdon or Jazzi."

"They could have paid someone to do it," Zandra said.

"With the bailiffs knocking at their door, where would they get those kinds of funds?" I asked. "Dark magic doesn't come cheap because the person who casts it bears a heavy burden."

"They could have gotten lucky and mixed together a successful spell," Zandra said. "Or they have a friend who owed them a favor."

I nodded as I considered the options. "Their home felt empty of magic. In fact, the whole of

Badger's Haze felt like it was decaying and had lost all hope."

"Because of the curse," Zandra said. "Hope was sucked out of that place a long time ago. Sometimes, when magic gets so twisted, there's nothing that can save it. Magic users abandon the place and let nature take over."

"I suppose so. But if you stay in a place like that long enough, you become a husk, too. Why do Langdon and Jazzi stay?"

"The inherited house," Zandra said. "All they have to do is pay the bills and the taxes."

"Which they haven't managed," I said. "And the bailiff will be leaving with empty hands."

"Finn will get to the bottom of it once he's separated Jazzi and Langdon and gotten one of them to talk," Zandra said.

"He may not have to. If the doctors fix Charlie, he'll identify the attacker, and this will all be over."

"And then everything will go back to normal."

I glanced at Zandra. "Including Tempest?"

"That's what I'm hoping. She'll be fine. We all have our off days."

I huffed out a soft breath. I didn't want to burden Zandra with my concerns about Tempest, but I shared the same worries as Wiggles. Tempest was acting out of character, and when a witch with so much power went wonky, you kept your guard up or you didn't survive.

Zandra pulled up outside the hospital, and we climbed out. She went inside first, then headed back out and let me know which room Charlie was in and the window to aim for. A few moments later, I hopped through an open window and found myself in a neat, white, private hospital room.

"We've got five minutes." Zandra kept her voice low. "The nurse said there's been no change, but Charlie's not to be bothered or stressed. We need to keep everything calm."

Charlie lay flat on his back in the hospital bed. There was a powerful ward of shimmering magic covering him. It must be a restore or remedy spell used to counteract whatever had struck him down.

"Did the nurse tell you if he's been conscious?" I asked.

"She said they struggled to get him stable, and they're keeping him heavily sedated until they can figure out what happened."

"There were no clues? Cythera said the tests run on Erick's body were inconclusive."

Zandra shook her head. "Looking at the state Charlie's in, he'll be no help in figuring out what happened."

"He must have tried to help Erick and got hurt."

"Perhaps he was collateral damage." Zandra's mobile globe buzzed, and she pulled it out of her pocket. "Hey! This is progress. Langdon wants to confess!"

"Success! Let's get back to Angel Force."

Zandra tilted her head. "I wonder what the angels said to make him change his mind?"

"They could have offered a deal," I said. "Or maybe Jazzi has evidence that's so damning, Langdon had no choice but to confess."

"Whatever it is, let's go find out." Zandra headed out the main door while I hopped out the window and hurried back to the van.

We were soon back at Angel Force, eager to hear the news and clear Tempest's name.

"You don't need to be here." Cythera was skulking around the office, looking like she wanted to cause trouble.

"But here we are, happy and willing to take part," I said. "And I hear there's a confession about to be made."

"Finn said you'd want to listen in. Go in the room next door. I don't want you in the interview."

We swiftly settled in the room with the one-way mirror and a listening device so we could hear what Langdon had to say.

"There's got to be a deal to be made if you expect me to tell you everything," Langdon said.

Finn shook his head as Cythera entered the room and rejoined the interview. "You're confessing to a serious crime. That doesn't get you any kind of deal."

"It's not that serious!" Langdon said. "But I don't want my guilt to make you think I'm a killer."

"You are," Cythera said. "You told us you wanted to confess."

"So I don't keep getting nervous and mess up my words," Langdon said. "I'm bad with words. They stick in my head and come out wrong from my mouth. It gets me in trouble."

"There'll be no deals," Cythera said. "With Erick dead and Charlie on the critical list, it's likely you'll have not one, but two murders on your charge sheet."

"No! You don't get it," Langdon said. "I'm not confessing to that. I'm innocent of murder. That's way too messy for my style."

"But you said you wanted to make a confession," Finn said. "We brought you in here because we're concerned about your involvement in your brother's death."

"I know! But I want to confess to another crime," Langdon said. "You're grilling me, and it's making me panic and worry you'll find out the truth."

"The truth about what?" Cythera asked through gritted teeth.

Langdon ran a hand down his face. "I don't have much luck holding down a job, so money's tight. But I found a solution to help me get by. The problem is, it's not legal."

"What do you do?" Finn asked.

"I've been making and selling counterfeit love potions and charms. I know it's wrong, and I'm messing with people's dreams of getting a happily ever after, but I need the cash. It's been weighing on my mind, and all this questioning has made me feel guilty. That's what I wanted to confess to. With a clear head, I won't put my foot in it."

Zandra groaned. "Is he for real?"

"Langdon strikes me as a simple character," I said. "I understand why he'd be panicking and wracked with guilt over conning lonely hearts out of money."

"He's just wasted our time!" Zandra said.

"I promise you I had nothing to do with what happened to Erick," Langdon said. "The only one mean enough to kill in our family is Jazzi. She did it. And I can prove it."

Cythera flared her wings. "So prove it! Tell us what you know."

"Not here." Langdon shook his head. "To show Jazzi is guilty, you need to take me home."

Chapter 17

Manifesting

"Take me with you." Langdon trailed Cythera around the office like a baby dragon when he knew there were treats tucked into a pocket. "The evidence is hidden. You'll never find it without me. I can be helpful."

"Tell me what this evidence is that proves your sister's guilt. My team is more than capable of finding anything." Cythera turned so abruptly that Langdon almost walked into her. "If you keep information from us during an active investigation, it gives me grounds to lock you up. And I already have reasons to do that, so don't make this easy for me."

"I can't stay in a cage! I love my freedom. You confine me to a cell, and I'll wither. I don't like ties or routine, you see. I'm a free bird."

"Langdon will have to get used to a harsh routine if he's charged with Erick's murder," Zandra muttered to me.

I nodded. We'd been watching the begging routine ever since Langdon's declaration he could show us Jazzi was guilty of murder.

Jazzi knew nothing about this revelation, having been tucked away in another interview room, but she'd be furious when she found out Langdon was attempting to clear his name by smearing hers.

"Let's take him to the house," I said. "You won't do anything foolish, will you, Langdon?"

"I'm not known for my smarts, but I know when to behave. I respect law enforcement. I want my brother's killer found, too. What they did to him was wrong."

"What you did to him," Cythera said.

"Uh-uh. Not me."

"It was wrong to stick Erick's face to your dartboard," Zandra said.

Langdon's cheeks flushed. "I already said I meant nothing by that. I was just fooling around. Erick thought it was fun, too."

This guy's life appeared to be one giant joke. But this time, it had backfired on him.

"I'll come, too," Finn said. "That way, one of us can look around the house while the other watches Langdon."

"You don't need to watch me. When we get back, I need to eat, though. I'm starving. It must be the stress. Stress makes you hungry, doesn't it?" Langdon asked.

Cythera let out an exasperated sigh. "You'd better not be messing us around. I'll have you put away for wasting Angel Force's time. And I'll take pleasure in doing so."

"I'll show you everything you need to prove Jazzi did it," Langdon said.

"It would be convenient if she did," I murmured to Zandra. "With Jazzi behind bars, Langdon can move back into the house and turn it into one large party den, with no nagging from his sister."

"I doubt they'll have a house for much longer," she replied. "I got a glimpse of that letter. They have a huge debt hanging over them."

"Langdon is a live in the moment guy, though. He can only tackle one problem at a time. First, he gets the house, then he figures out the debt issue."

"He could burn it down and claim the insurance," Zandra said.

We smirked. Those two wouldn't have insurance for anything.

After a few minutes of Cythera striding around, barking orders, and getting things arranged, we left Angel Force and returned to Jazzi and Langdon's house. The angels flew, and we took Langdon in the van.

"These are great wheels," Langdon said. "Sturdy. Get the job done."

"I work at animal control," Zandra said. "This van is a perk of the job."

"Tough work. Ever get bitten?"

"Not with me around," I said.

"You're a feisty little dudette, aren't you?" Langdon attempted to scratch behind my ears.

I moved out of his way. I enjoyed a good scratch, but he was a murder suspect, so it felt wrong to be petted by him.

He raised a hand. "I get it. Boundaries. Personal space. I always forget that kind of thing. I don't have to worry about it when I'm in my garage. I can play my games and lose myself in another world. Sometimes, life is easier that way. Real stuff is hard. People can be mean. Jazzi is always mean. I'm surprised she hasn't killed before. She's threatened to enough times. She once chased me along the street with a frying pan. She wanted to knock my head off."

"Was that why you burned down her kitchen?" I asked.

"Oh! No. She chased me because I used her face cream on my gross foot skin. You know how you can get a build-up and it all cracks? Nasty. She found out and yelled at me for ages."

"Life isn't always easy," I said. "There are often troubles that need smoothing."

"Yeah. My sister causes most of mine," Langdon said. "I always wondered when she'd snap. I never figured it would be so bad that she'd kill Erick, though."

"What's this evidence you've got on her?" Zandra asked.

Langdon grimaced. "You have to see it to believe it. I was shocked when I found it. Almost as shocked as when I opened the drawer beside her bed. A brother should never see things like that."

"How did you find this evidence?" Zandra asked.

"I was just looking around. After all, it's my house, too, even though Jazzi tells me I don't deserve it and took my keys. I was looking for clean socks. I'd been turning my old pairs inside out to get another wear out of them, but they were standing up on their own. Jazzi buys the most amazing soft socks. They're in weird colors, but I don't mind. I was hunting for socks when I found it."

"Found what?"

Langdon wasn't giving up his collateral. Although we tried several ways to find out what he had on Jazzi, he just kept shaking his head. He was acting more as if he were on a fun day out than about to be charged in a murder investigation.

I suppose it was a simpler way to live. Don't think about the past or the future. Focus on one breath at a time. Simple but not always sensible when trouble finds you.

Cythera and Finn were already at the house when we pulled up. We climbed out and joined them.

Langdon unlocked the front door using a hidden key under a plant pot, let us in, and led us to Jazzi's bedroom. He opened the closet, knocked a false panel off the back wall, and stepped back. "There you go. Jazzi's vision board."

We shuffled closer and discovered a large pinboard covered in images and motivational phrases, including: *Boss Girl Rules. Fake it Until You Make it. Dream Big, Love Hard.*

"You see?" Langdon said. "Everything on that board is what Erick had. And there's even a drawing of Erick. He's on his knees. Begging."

"How is this evidence Jazzi murdered Erick?" Cythera asked.

"Jazzi's deepest desires are on the board," Langdon said. "She was so envious of everything Erick had. The houses. The money. The good job.

She wanted it all. She wanted to take it from him. Jazzi manifested Erick's death. She made it happen because she killed him."

Cythera wrinkled her nose and stepped back from the closet. "Successful manifesting comes from having clear goals, planning how you'll achieve them, and then executing practical and manageable steps. There's nothing special about manifesting. You don't put a picture on a board and suddenly it happens. That's nonsense."

"There's something to be said for having a clear vision," I said. "If you focus on the thing you most desire, you're more likely to see an opportunity to get it when it arises."

"Manifesting doesn't work," Cythera said. "You can spend hours pinning things to boards. Your dream home. Your perfect job. Your ideal man. If that's all you do, you'll fail. You must take action on your dreams."

"It sounds like you have experience in this field," I said. "Did your vision board fail to come true? It can't be the ideal husband. You have Maverick, and he's charm personified."

"I've seen people write down lists and then try to magic it into reality," Cythera said. "All they get is disappointment and no closer to what they want. Hard work and dedication. That's what manifests what you desire. All this woo-woo nonsense makes people lazy."

"Jazzi sometimes acted on her desires," Langdon said. "She was obsessed with finding a guy to marry. That's her ideal man on the board. The one in the tuxedo with the dark hair."

"Jazzi was active in the dating scene," I said. "There you go, Cythera. Jazzi was taking practical steps to make her dreams come true."

"This vision board doesn't show Jazzi destroying anyone." Cythera sighed. "Let's suspend reality for a second and believe such trite nonsense works. Where is the image of Jazzi scaring Erick to death with magic?"

"He's on there! The guy on his knees. He's grovelling to Jazzi. That's Erick. Jazzi never thought Erick deserved any success. He was bookish and quiet when he was a kid, so he got teased."

"By you and Jazzi?" I asked.

"Only for fun," Langdon said. "Erick was an easy target. And you know what kids are like."

"They're mean," I said. "And that meanness sticks. It's fortunate Erick was able to overcome your unkind treatment and make something of his life."

Langdon lowered his head. "Erick always had his books and games as friends. I'm the same these days. When I've had a tough day, I put on a game, down a few beers, and I become the game character. They have way cooler lives."

"This is a waste of time," Cythera said. "It's clear neither you nor Jazzi liked Erick. You both have motives for wanting him dead. Confess you did it together, and I'll see about making that deal."

"But... but I was with my buddies," Langdon said. "I was in my garage all night."

"Jazzi said you were missing when she checked on you," Cythera said.

"Not true! Speak to my buddies," Langdon said. "They'll tell you I was there."

"They won't tell us anything of use since they were passed out drunk or high on whatever substances you were enjoying," Cythera replied. "No doubt, illegal substances that'll get you in even more trouble. Should I organize a search of your garage and find more problems for you?"

Shock paled Langdon's face. "I just like a good time. I had no issue with Erick."

I wanted to believe Langdon, and his surprise at Cythera's assertions seemed sincere, but he had a poor relationship with Erick, and there had been issues between them that went back years. Langdon was a plausible suspect.

"What can I do to get you to see sense?" Langdon asked. "This vision board has to mean something. Talk to Jazzi and tell her what you know. Maybe you can get her to crack."

"We'll be speaking to both of you again," Cythera said. "And we'll be checking your alibis. We'll also be speaking to neighbors. Perhaps one of them saw you leave the party on your way to Crimson Cove."

"Crimson where? I wouldn't know where that is," Langdon said. "And I have zero sense of direction."

"You don't need directions to use a translocation spell," Cythera said.

"That magic is way beyond me. If I need to get anywhere, I walk, ride my bike, or thumb a lift."

"What about the car sitting in your driveway?" I asked.

"That hunk of junk hasn't gone anywhere in months," Langdon said. "I can't afford to insure the thing, and it needs new tires. They don't come cheap."

While Langdon debated his innocence with Cythera, I wandered around Jazzi's bedroom. Was one of them lying to us? Were they hoping, if we couldn't prove for certain which one of them had done it, they'd go free? Or were they both guilty? Perhaps Erick had changed his mind about the house. Or they'd pushed him too far in their demands for money, so he confronted them and told them to leave him alone, so they got their revenge.

I was certain Tempest hadn't been involved in Erick's murder, and I'd swiftly ruled out Randal. And although Dilbert Dimitri had a motive, he had a solid alibi.

That left Langdon and Jazzi. It had to be them.

"You're making a huge mistake thinking I had anything to do with this," Langdon said. "I sell fake love, not real murder!"

Cythera didn't look convinced. "Finn, collect the vision board. We'll take it with us, though it proves nothing conclusive."

"Do I have to come back with you?" Langdon asked.

"Of course you do. You're wasting our time trying to distract us," Cythera said.

"At least let me get something to eat," Langdon said. "I can't think straight with an empty belly."

Once Finn had removed the vision board, Cythera grudgingly allowed Langdon to make a cheese sandwich, making sure to follow him closely in case he made a run for it, while we remained in Jazzi's bedroom.

"What's on your mind?" Zandra muttered to me. "Are you looking for something?"

"I feel as if we've missed a clue," I said.

"You don't think Langdon and Jazzi are guilty? They have motives and the time to get to Crimson Cove without being noticed."

"I'm unsure, and that's never a good thing."

"Better them be charged with Erick's murder than Tempest still in the frame."

"I agree." I hopped on the polycotton duvet cover. It needed to go into the washing machine. "But did we miss a clue?"

"I don't think so. What's got you worried?" Zandra asked.

"It's a feeling. I sense something bigger is at play, but I can't put my paw on what it is."

"Once we get a confession from Langdon or Jazzi, this will all be over," Zandra said. "There's no need to make things more complicated. Sibling rivalry can be intense. I know. I had my fair share of it with Tempest."

Perhaps Zandra was right. I'd be sure to check Langdon and Jazzi's alibis myself. It was important we got the right person off the streets. Otherwise, a dangerous killer would remain on the loose. And someone with that kind of power running through their veins, using it to destroy, was a danger to all of us.

Finn walked back into the bedroom after stashing the vision board in Zandra's van. "Cythera intends to hold Langdon and Jazzi for twenty-four hours. We'll interview them again and speak to Jazzi about her vision board."

"Which one of them did it?" Zandra asked.

Finn pinched his chin between his thumb and forefinger. "I'm not convinced it was either of them. They're not upstanding citizens, but you need to be passionate, insane, or highly motivated to end someone's life. Langdon is a good-time guy who lives in the moment, and Jazzi seems focused only on finding a boyfriend. I can't see either of them being bothered enough to kill Erick."

"Juno thinks the same," Zandra said. "But I'd rather Cythera keep her suspicious eye on them instead of poking Tempest. She gets angry when the angels mess with her."

"We all know better than to hassle a Crypt witch." Finn smiled at Zandra. "We need to catch the killer, though."

"We'll leave no stone unturned," I said. "While Cythera deals with Erick's family, we'll get to work and discover if anything or anyone has been overlooked."

Chapter 18

Alibis analyzed

"That must be him." I sat upright in the late-night café chair as a tall, handsome, dark-haired man strode toward the table. We'd been waiting for Ruben Silver for half an hour.

"He looks just like the guy on Jazzi's vision board." Zandra stifled a yawn. "Although she failed to manifest his decent timekeeping skills."

After we'd searched Jazzi's home and discovered her vision board, we'd returned to Angel Force. Finn had gathered details on Jazzi's disastrous date and contacted Langdon's party buddies. To save time, we split the tasks, tackling them separately to get answers as to whether Jazzi or Langdon were behind Erick's murder.

"Zandra?" Ruben stopped close to our table, his eyebrows raised.

"Good guess," she said.

"You're the only ones in here. And you said you'd be with your cat familiar." He held out a hand, which she shook. "I'm sorry to keep you waiting. I was on a date, and it was tricky to get away."

"Greetings," I said. "You sound like you have a full dating calendar."

Ruben shrugged off his jacket, settled it on the back of the seat, and then sat. "You've got to put yourself out there to find your perfect woman."

"Which is why we're here," I said.

Ruben raised a hand and ordered himself a decaf coffee. "Do either of you want anything?"

"I've already had two coffees while we were waiting," Zandra said.

"Nothing for me," I added.

"I can't handle anything caffeinated this late," Ruben said. "It's a sign of getting old. When I was in my twenties, I could down several espressos at midnight, and they'd have no negative impact."

"We need to take care of our bodies," I said. "They're the only ones we get."

"I do, generally. Eat healthy most of the time. Although all this wining and dining to find my soulmate plays havoc with the waistline."

"Tell us about your date with Jazzi," I said.

"I was interested when you mentioned her when you made contact," Ruben said. "Jazzi didn't leave the best impression, and I didn't hide my disappointment well enough. I wondered..."

"Go on," I prompted.

"Well, some ladies can be unkind and make unfounded complaints when a date doesn't go their way."

"Why would she complain about you?" I asked.

Ruben's coffee arrived, and he paused to take a sip. "I've been dating for the last year. I wouldn't say I'm picky, but I have a type. When I read Jazzi's profile, she sounded perfect. We chatted a few times, and I liked what I heard."

"But when you met, you realized she hadn't been honest with you?" Zandra asked.

"Some women—and not all women, most of you are great—put on an act to make you think they're your ideal woman. They say they like the same things as you. Same music, hobbies, food, vacations. They pretend they're interested in your career. I'm always suspicious of women like that. If you mold yourself to fit into someone else's life, you're not being your authentic self, and you can only fake things for so long before your true self shows through."

"What happens then?" I asked.

Ruben grimaced. "That's when the problems appear. You discover you've been tricked, and the woman gets frustrated because she's pretending to be something she's not. I believe there's a soulmate out there for everyone, so there's no need to fake who you are. You'll find each other, eventually."

"Some of us are happy being single," Zandra said.

"You haven't found your soulmate?" Ruben asked.

"My career keeps me busy. As does this sideline. As I mentioned, Jazzi's brother Erick was murdered. Jazzi is a suspect."

Ruben's easy smile faded. "I've already spoken to Angel Force about that. I went on a date with Jazzi on the night her brother died. Usually, the dates go on until late, but I ended things early. I could tell we weren't a match. It was disappointing, but there was no point in wasting time or leading Jazzi on. It's cruel to give a lady false hope."

"We heard you ditched Jazzi before dessert and left her with the restaurant bill," I said.

Ruben's cheeks flushed. "It wasn't my proudest moment. I had a headache and an upset stomach, so I didn't want anything else to eat. I kept saying I didn't feel well and needed to leave, but Jazzi pressured me to stay. She said she could be my dessert. Honestly, that turned my stomach even more."

"It's still not polite to ditch someone," I said. "Jazzi has her faults, but it was rude."

"Yes, it was. I should apologize. Although, if I send her flowers as an apology gift, she'll think I'm interested, and I don't want to give her the wrong impression." Ruben sighed. "It's so difficult to know which way to step, even what to say on a date, in case the other person takes offense or gets the wrong idea."

"Just leave her a message and say you acted like a jerk and didn't mean to hurt her feelings," Zandra said.

"Yes, I could do that. Or maybe you could tell her. After all, if Jazzi killed her brother, she's not safe to be around. I don't want to make myself vulnerable to attack, especially since she already has issues with me because of the whole awkward date situation."

Zandra stifled another yawn. My witch's energy was waning, so we needed to wrap this up and find out what Finn learned from Langdon's party buddies.

"During the date, did Jazzi say or do anything to make you uncomfortable?" I asked. "Other than putting on a persona you saw straight through."

"Nothing that would make me think she was a killer," Ruben said. "And believe me, I've been on a few dates where I've had doubts about the woman's sanity. And that's not a joke. Jazzi was pleasant enough. She laughed at my terrible jokes. But she had no depth. When I asked about her future plans, she had none. I like a woman with substance. There's no point in being with someone who lives their life through you. Dependency is a dangerous trait in any relationship."

"Being too independent also has its downsides." I glanced at Zandra.

"You need balance," Ruben replied. "Jazzi had no balance. I learned all I wanted to know quickly, and since I wasn't feeling well, I planned my exit. When Jazzi made that difficult, I slipped away. For all her faults, I got no sense she was unstable."

"What about her powers?" I asked.

"When we talked about her magic, she said she rarely used it. She told me it often skips generations or is much weaker in some of her family members. She mentioned another brother who had little ability, too. The brother who died, Erick, wasn't it? He got all the talent."

"When Jazzi spoke about Erick, how did she sound?" I asked.

"She didn't mention her family much. I got the impression there was jealousy there, though. She sneered when she mentioned what Erick did for a career. I thought it sounded impressive. My magic is basic level, but it does the job. Anyone with advanced skills is always fascinating to me."

"What time did you sneak off from your date?" Zandra asked.

"We had a late dinner," Ruben said. "We met at nine and were finished about an hour and a half later. I was home by eleven."

"Did Jazzi contact you after the date to see why you left?" I asked.

"No. I was worried she might, since she had my number. We met on a dating app, so when I got home, I removed her from my favorites list."

"How many favorites do you have on that list?" I asked.

"Far fewer than I'd like," Ruben said. "I hoped my actions would send the appropriate message without causing too much hurt."

"Do you know how long Jazzi waited for you at the restaurant?"

"It closed at midnight." Ruben's eyes widened. "I hope she wasn't waiting all that time. I'd feel terrible if she did. I'm not that much of a catch!"

This was interesting news and supported Langdon's theory that Jazzi had an opportunity to get to Crimson Cove and kill Erick.

"Did Jazzi mention ever visiting a town called Crimson Cove?" I asked.

"No, and we talked about vacation plans. She said she liked beach holidays or lazing around the pool. I'm an adventure man. She didn't mention taking any city breaks or short trips. What's so special about Crimson Cove?"

"It's where Erick was killed," Zandra said.

"Oh! I see." Ruben sipped more coffee. "I can give you the contact information for the restaurant so you can check exactly when Jazzi left."

"That would be good," Zandra said. Her mobile snow globe buzzed, and she checked it. "Finn's done."

"I hope you figure out what happened to Erick," Ruben said. "If it was Jazzi, then I had a near miss."

"Thanks for your time," I said. "Good luck with your dating."

Ruben finished his coffee and smiled. "Good luck with your search for justice."

We said our goodbyes, and Ruben left.

"If you're too tired, we can call it a night," I said to Zandra.

"I'm good. This has been a hectic few days, though. We're neglecting everything."

"Nothing is as important as this."

"I can think of one thing." Zandra tapped her bare wrist where my bracelet gift used to sit. An enchanted bracelet.

"This must take priority. Tempest is still in the frame for murder." I jumped onto her shoulder. "Let's get back to Crimson Cove and see what Finn discovered."

We drove back in silence, Zandra yawning repeatedly, while I turned over everything Ruben had told us. It looked bad for Jazzi, but I still wasn't convinced it was her. Everything about her life screamed lackluster: her tired house, the kitchen still smoke-damaged from the fire, her lack of employment, even her dating history. Finn was right—killing took effort, and I couldn't imagine

Jazzi putting in the amount of effort needed to make it happen.

We found Finn back at Angel Force. He was slouched in his chair, a mug of tea in one hand and a chocolate cookie in the other.

Zandra grabbed a cookie of her own while I settled on Finn's desk. "How did you get on with Langdon's friends?"

"They did their best, but they admitted they had a lot to drink that night. None of them could be sure on the timings," Finn said. "They also all fell asleep at various points during the evening."

"Giving Langdon time to slip off and kill Erick?"

"His alibi is poor," Finn said. "It's easy to pick holes in it. How about you?"

"The same with Jazzi," I said. "From the timings her date gave us, it would have been easy for her to get here."

"So, they both had the opportunity."

"But we still have doubts about them, don't we?" I asked.

"We should sleep on it," Finn said. "Maybe new information will show up tomorrow. I found an old social media profile for Erick, and there were pictures of a girlfriend. Nothing recent posted about their relationship, but I thought I'd do some digging, see if anything useful turns up."

"Check with the restaurant Jazzi and Ruben dined at, too," I said. "I don't see any reason why Ruben would have lied about what time he abandoned Jazzi, but it may help us pin down the timings."

"I'll get on that first thing in the morning," Finn said. "Now, take Zandra home. She can barely keep her eyes open."

Zandra waved away the comment. "I'm fine."

"We've done enough for tonight," I said. "With fresh eyes, we'll get to the bottom of this mystery tomorrow."

I was awoken by a set of needle claws digging into my tail. I yelped and flipped over to find all three kittens sitting at the bottom of Zandra's bed, their eyes alight with mischief.

"Behave! That's not how you treat your elders. And definitely not how you wake them."

The kittens bounced about then dashed off up the basement stairs before I could box them with my paws.

What an unwelcome wake-up call! I checked my tail for injuries then rolled over and stretched. Head. Neck. Spine. Tail. Back legs. Front legs. Purrfection.

"What's going on?" Zandra mumbled, face down on her pillow.

"The kittens are bored. Or hungry. They're bouncing around again."

"I need coffee." Zandra rolled out of bed, stood, and did a stretch similar to mine, her fingers almost brushing the ceiling.

I waited a few minutes while she dressed and groomed herself, then we went up to the kitchen.

Vorana was there, along with Tempest and Wiggles. There was no sign of Sage. It was unusual for her not to be in the kitchen when Vorana was in there, but perhaps she'd had enough of the kittens jumping on her. And she still hadn't forgiven them for setting fire to her prickly mat.

"There you are!" Vorana said. "There's nothing cooked this morning. The electrics are still wonky. I'm getting someone in to take a look."

"Cold breakfast?" Zandra wrinkled her nose.

"Don't blame me! Blame the house being on the fritz." Vorana had laid out a selection of delicious-looking pastries, fruit, and plenty of coffee. Of course, there was delectable smoked salmon for me and Sage.

"How's the investigation going?" Tempest asked. "I could do with getting back to Willow Tree Falls today."

"We're stuck between two suspects," I said. "Erick's brother and sister, Langdon and Jazzi."

"Did they do it?" Vorana joined us at the table.

"It's possible, although I'm not convinced," I said. "Their alibis are as wonky as your electrics. Cythera is keeping them in a cell until we can dig up the truth. She's not happy."

"I doubt that angel of yours is ever happy," Tempest muttered as a small kitten fireball shot over her head.

"Behave!" I shot a withering look at the kittens as they continued sparking magic and play fighting. "Tempest, you're supposed to be keeping an eye on those kittens."

"I am! But they're free spirits. And they keep vanishing. I think they can already translocate."

"They're too small to have control over such a spell."

"They have way too much power." Tempest ducked another fireball.

One kitten launched itself onto the table and knocked over a mug of coffee.

"They have so much energy." Vorana mopped up the mess. "And they barely sleep. We really need to find somewhere they can be properly trained. Poor Sage is hiding most of the time to avoid them. I haven't seen her since last night."

I scarfed down the last of my smoked salmon. "I'll find Sage. And Tempest, take Wiggles and the kittens for a walk. Be careful, though. Cythera saw Wiggles out with the kittens, and she says they've been causing trouble."

"As if I'd take those fluffy fire starters anywhere," Wiggles said. "They were stalking me! I was minding my own business yesterday, and one of those little goons bit me on the butt."

"Whatever you're up to, stay under the radar." I hopped off the chair. "And kittens, no more biting or shooting out fireballs."

I got answered with hisses. Feisty little critters. I headed outside to get fresh air and hunt for Sage. There was no sign of her under any of the bushes she liked to snooze by, but there was noise coming from one of Vorana's sheds.

I pulled open the door with a paw. Sage was bundled in some old fishing net. It was wrapped around her head, and her paws were so tightly tangled they were pinned to her sides.

She hissed when she saw me and squirmed about. "Get me out of here!"

I dashed over and yanked her free from the net. She flopped onto her side, panting.

"What happened?" I asked.

"I... I don't remember. I got zapped by a spell, and that was it! I came to in the shed in the early hours of the morning. I could barely move. That binding was cutting off my air supply. I'd be dead if I hadn't chewed through a small section."

"Who did this to you?" I inspected a ragged hole in the netting.

Sage heaved out a sigh. "I have enemies. Perhaps they've finally found me."

"You do?"

"From a long time ago. Before I knew you," she said. "I had a reputation."

"You still do. Let me help you up. You're freezing, and you must be hungry."

"Starving! I expect those despicable kittens have eaten all my kibble." Sage nudged me with her head. "Promise me you won't tell Vorana you found me like this."

"She needs to know if someone is after you," I said.

"Vorana can't know! She'll think I'm not good enough or unable to protect her since I ended up in this mess."

"You protect each other," I said. "If you've got an old enemy after you, you need someone watching your back. Vorana is that perfect someone."

"You watch my back. This stays between us, got it?"

I huffed out my frustration but nodded. I was worried. Was my dear friend at risk?

Chapter 19

Catch up

Despite attempts to get more information from Sage, she remained stubbornly silent about the attack and simply demanded I tell no one about how I found her.

Concern still lingered that she had a powerful enemy after her, but I also wondered if she was embarrassed about being caught. Sage often napped in strange places, and since her favorite spot in the kitchen had been destroyed, thanks to the feisty kittens, it wasn't out of the realm of possibility that Sage had rolled into the netting and gotten caught. But why hadn't she used magic to free herself?

It was yet another puzzle to add to the list of mysteries I was dealing with. And all those puzzles had to wait while I crammed several days of work at animal control into a single shift to make up for our recent absence.

Zandra leaned back in her seat and blew out a long breath. She twisted her hands around to ease her wrist joints. "So many forms! It seems like there are more forms than actual animal rescues these days."

I hopped onto her desk and settled on a comfortable stack of papers. "We've been out of the loop while we focus on clearing Tempest's name. The paperwork soon stacks up."

Zandra looked at her mobile snow globe and frowned. "There's been no word from Angel Force and nothing from Tempest. I know she wants to leave town, but she'll find herself in trouble if she leaves before Cythera gives her the okay to go."

I gently rubbed a paw over my ear. "How did Tempest seem to you this morning?"

"The same as always."

"I sensed something different about her," I said. "Not so much now, but I wondered if maybe Tempest was struggling with her power."

"The family carries strong magic," Zandra said. "I don't have to deal with it because I don't have the Crypt witch blood, but I was exposed to the same spells and learned how to control most of the powers. It must be exhausting, having all that energy and needing to keep on top of it."

"You excel with your magic," I said. "You're a proud addition to that family."

"I get by." Zandra looked over as the door opened and Finn entered our office.

"Greetings! Have Langdon and Jazzi confessed?" I asked.

"No, they're being stubborn," Finn said. "Even when we showed Jazzi the vision board, she wouldn't budge. She yelled for several minutes about her private space being invaded and tarnishing her manifestations. Cythera wasn't happy when Jazzi threatened to file a complaint and demanded to meet with a higher angel."

"But you have news?" I asked.

He nodded. "I did some digging overnight. I focused on Erick's old girlfriend, the one I saw in the online pictures. Karina Bellow. I interviewed a few of her friends, and they said in the last few days, she's been behaving strangely."

"A murderous kind of strange?" Zandra asked.

"Weird. Hard to communicate with," Finn said. "I tried to get in touch with her, but she hasn't responded to my messages. I also visited her home, but she wasn't there. And the place she works at hasn't seen her for days."

"Is that unusual?" I asked. "Is Karina considered reliable?"

"She is. This is where things get even weirder," Finn said. "Karina has been spotted around Crimson Cove."

"The former girlfriend came after Erick?" I asked. "Did their relationship end badly?"

"I asked Karina's friends about it, but they said it just fizzled out. Karina wanted to get serious with Erick, but he was only interested in his work. And then another woman came on the scene, so Karina backed away. She'd had enough of fighting for something when it was clear she had no chance of winning."

"Erick didn't have a girlfriend," I said. "So who's the other woman?"

"I couldn't get that information," Finn said. "But I want to go after Karina. I need to know if she was in Crimson Cove the night Erick was killed."

The atmosphere electrified, and there was a haze of magic that sent a shimmer of power around the office. Granny Dottie appeared, her gray hair awry and her cheeks flushed. There was a ragged slash in her jacket. "Good! I found you. We have a problem."

"We're working on solving the murder as quickly as we can," I said.

"Not that! There's been another breakout at the demon prison. I'm here to collect Tempest. We need all hands on deck. I tried the house, but you've got some powerful wards around it, and my magic wouldn't get through. I knew this was where you worked. You need to get me to Tempest."

"She can't leave Crimson Cove," I said. "The angels will arrest her."

"We need her power!" Granny Dottie said. "The demons aren't messing around. I don't know how they're doing it, but they keep breaking through the prison barriers. The magic is warping and fading."

"I'll come with you. I know the prison wards almost as well as Tempest." Zandra stood from her desk. "Juno, stay with Finn. Find Erick's old girlfriend and see what she has to say for herself."

"I don't want you going up against a pack of demons on your own," I said.

Granny Dottie grunted and cracked her knuckles. "She won't be alone. We're all there. But there's a lot of ground to cover, and some of the ward breaches need guarding to make sure no more demons get out."

"Give Zandra the least dangerous task you can," I insisted.

"I can handle a few demons," Zandra said, with an eye roll. "I trained with Tempest, remember?"

"As if I could forget," I said. "Stay safe."

Granny Dottie grabbed Zandra's hand, and they vanished in a flash of magic.

Finn opened the office door. "Zandra knows how to look after herself. I've seen her deal with heaps of nasties. Even me when my demon power gets unstable."

"I want to be with her," I said. "It feels wrong to be separated."

"You'll be back together before you know it. The sooner we find Karina and see if she's behind what happened to Erick, the faster you'll be reunited and can go bite some demons."

"I rarely bite them. They taste foul. Is Karina still in Crimson Cove?" I followed Finn as he headed to the exit.

"Location spells have come up with nothing, so I was going to try her hometown, Rainbow Hollow."

"It sounds charming," I said.

"It's a tourist hotspot. Pretty, but avoid it during the holidays. It's a half-hour drive or a ten-minute flight."

I grimaced. I wasn't a fan of flying with the angels, but at least flying with Finn meant I'd keep warm. "Let's take to the wing. The quicker, the better."

Once we were outside, Finn tucked me carefully against his chest then shot into the air. I was surrounded by warm feathers and an unfamiliar woodland scent.

228

"Are you wearing a new cologne?" I asked.

Finn chuckled. "Bell got it as a gift for our one-month anniversary. I like it. The smell reminds me of her. She spends so much time with the dragons these days, so she always smells like a grove of trees with a hint of smoke."

"I'm glad you found each other," I said. "And I'm happy Bell is flourishing with the dragons."

"They keep her on her toes, that's for sure," Finn said. "But the realm is at peace, and it's all thanks to her."

"I believe we had a small part to play in that stability," I said. "I'm just glad there was a successful resolution."

"I'm figuring out how to split my time between the two places," Finn said. "I don't want Bell to leave when she's so happy, so I'm hoping to reduce my hours at Angel Force and hire someone to look after the animal sanctuary. If you know anyone who's looking to deal with grumpy, often snappy magical creatures, let me know."

"Are you talking about Cythera?"

He laughed. "I can't pay much, but I'll throw in free accommodation at the sanctuary."

"It would take a unique and special person to take on that job," I said.

"Let's hope they're out there."

Finn swooped lower, and soon we were flying over the pretty parish of Rainbow Hollow. It was clearly a magical town. There were faint sparkles of magic drifting into the air, releasing a sweet cinnamon scent.

"That doesn't look healthy." I gestured to a plume of smoke billowing from a small house set close to a grove of trees.

"That could be Karina's handiwork." Finn landed, keeping me close against him until it was safe for me to drop to the ground. "She's an elemental witch with a knack for fire. A friend said her powers have been unstable. Things keep exploding whenever she's around."

"Perhaps that's why she's not been at work and is avoiding people," I said. "If her powers are going haywire, she won't want to harm anyone."

"Or is she hiding because she's guilty of murder?" Finn asked. "There's something else you need to know about her. Karina is a hag-shifter. She can change to look like an original hag."

I sucked in a breath. "Claws for fingernails, serrated teeth, and glowing green eyes?"

"The originals weren't pretty, but they were powerful and merciless," Finn said. "Karina's ancestors were hags, but they thought they'd gotten rid of the magic by being careful about who they married. They failed. The magical genes didn't disappear. They simply skipped a few generations and landed in Karina."

"Is Karina scary enough to terrify someone to death?" We were walking toward the house fire, where a small crowd had gathered.

"It could explain what happened to Erick," Finn said. "Karina wanted him back. She tracked him to Crimson Cove and approached him. When he said no, she transformed into a hag."

"And Erick died in terror. That would explain why your tests came back inconclusive."

"We wouldn't have tested for hag magic. It's rare."

"With good reason."

There were more cries of alarm, and several people from the crowd watching the burning building dashed off.

"What's going on?" Finn asked as we reached the group.

"Buildings keep catching fire," a short, brown-faced woman said, her beady eyes intent on the blaze.

"Who's doing this?" I asked.

She looked down at me and frowned. "You're not from around here?"

"We're investigating a case, and these fires could be connected to it," I said. "Anything you can tell us would be helpful."

The woman glanced at Finn.

"This is official Angel Force business," he said, offering her a calm smile. "We're following a lead on Karina Bellow. Do you know her?"

"Oh! Yes. Some people are saying she's causing these fires. I know Karina. I run the mobile library, and she comes in every week to get a new book. She's sweet. She wouldn't do this."

"When was the last time you saw her?" Finn asked.

The woman's forehead furrowed. "It's been several weeks, actually. I hope she's not unwell."

"If she caused this fire, it suggests she's nearby," I said to Finn. "Where will we find her?"

"If Karina is doing this, just follow the path of destruction," the woman said. "There are more fires as you get near the stores."

We headed in the direction a group of men had run. Another building was on fire, which they were working to extinguish. I caught a flash of movement zoom out of the building and over the chimney stack and chased after it, Finn close behind me.

A figure landed and shook out long, waist-length, matted dark hair. She was muttering words I couldn't make out.

"Karina Bellow?" Finn called out. "Stay where you are. We need to ask you some questions about Erick Farten."

She made no move to suggest she'd heard Finn. He repeated himself several times, but she stood there, her shoulders tense, her hands clenching and unclenching, the claw-like nails growing longer by the second.

"We're here to help," I said. "You're in trouble. I'm sure you didn't mean to start these fires. And you loved Erick. You didn't want to hurt him. You lost control."

Finally, and very slowly, she turned around. An original hag was a nightmare given form. Her appearance so twisted it clawed its way into the minds of anyone unlucky enough to cross her path. Her skin was ashen and cracked. Her eyes glowed a sickly, unnatural green that pierced any shadow.

If you were unlucky enough to meet an original hag by surprise, you froze in place, rooted by terror, heart pounding so hard it felt as if it would break free from your chest. Some found themselves unable to look away, trapped by the horror, while others ran as primal survival instincts took over.

When you met a hag, the safest, most sensible thing to do was walk away. But we couldn't.

Finn had taken several steps back when Karina turned her attention to us. His breathing was shallow, and his hands were in fists as he stared at her.

"I understand your desire to flee," I said. "But if Karina murdered Erick, we need to find a way to bring her in."

"I've never faced a hag before," he said.

"Then prepare for this to get messy. She'll be hellbent on destruction. So full of rage, she won't be reasoned with."

The air buzzed with tension as Karina's gaze locked onto us, her serrated teeth bared in a twisted, almost broken grin.

Finn and I exchanged a quick look. He was steeling himself, a flicker of his demon energy twisting around his white wings.

Karina's claw-like nails extended, and she hissed something in a guttural language that sent a chill down my spine. With a flick of her hand, she conjured blackened fire that rolled toward us like a breaking wave.

Finn thrust his hands forward to create a barrier of golden light. The fire splashed against it, sizzling and popping, but the force of it sent him staggering back, leaving scorch marks where it hit.

He gritted his teeth, wings bursting from his back in a flurry of white and dark feathers. He took to the air, rising above Karina's head, and threw a spear of radiant energy down at her. Karina let out a laugh, her voice cracking and raw as she absorbed the blow. Her skin smoked where the spear had hit, but she barely seemed to notice.

I called on my magic, channeling energy through my murder mittens. I leaped, claws outstretched, and swiped at Karina's legs, sending a pulse of magic that tangled around her feet.

She stumbled, but her strength was terrifying, and she tore through the bindings as if they were paper. Her fingers twisted as she cast a spell. Shadows coiled around me, and for a moment, I couldn't move.

With a snarl, I broke free, but not before she'd grabbed Finn in midair and hurled him to the ground with a sickening thud. He groaned, his wings twitching as he struggled to get up.

My fur bristled, and I drew on my ancient power. Karina had hag magic, but my skills weren't too shabby.

Karina advanced on Finn, her hands crackling with dark, unstable energy. She was barely holding herself together, her face twisted in confusion and agony. I realized, with a pang of pity, that the magic was eating her alive as she wielded it against us.

I bolted toward her, gathering speed, then launched myself onto her back, biting down on her shoulder and releasing a concentrated burst of energy.

Karina spasmed under my power. I scrambled off as she staggered, swiping wildly at the air. Her nails sliced across my side, and I hissed, feeling the sting of the injury, but kept my focus.

Finn dragged himself up. He spread his wings wide, and the air thickened with charged energy. With a snap of his fingers, he released a blinding light that slammed into Karina, throwing her back against a tree and sending me flying.

She tried to get up, her form flickering and disintegrating at the edges, but her strength was waning. Her eyes found mine, hollow and lost. For a second, the hag faded, and I saw the broken woman, who desperately needed help.

"Karina, you must stop! We're here to help. We can save you from this power." I limped toward her. "Let it go!"

"Die. Die. You must all die. Kill you all!" She formed a swirling, chaotic orb that pulsed with dark energy.

Finn threw a lasso of light around her, and as it tightened, the orb of magic shattered, the energy dispersing in a flash that rocked the ground.

Karina slumped, her body sinking to the earth as the last of the hag magic faded. She gave me one final, haunting look before her head drooped, and she went still.

The village was silent, the smell of charred wood and smoke lingering in the air. A small crowd watched from a distance, their faces pale with shock and disbelief.

I padded over to Finn and leaned against his leg, both of us exhausted but alive. "I'd call that a confession, wouldn't you?"

Chapter 20

Hag revealed

The flight back to Angel Force was silent and slow. Finn's injuries troubled him, but he doggedly flapped his wings, holding Karina against his chest.

I'd positioned myself on Finn's back, close to his neck, and discreetly channeled my power into him to ensure we had a smooth ride. It was a windy position, and I was frozen by the time we got back to Crimson Cove, but given Karina's erratic and powerful magic, I hadn't wanted to risk using spells on her until she was in a secure environment.

Finn's landing was clumsy, but he stayed on his feet as we arrived outside Angel Force. Karina slumped forward, not having the strength to keep herself upright. Although perhaps it was a form of protest. She knew her days of freedom were numbered, so she was clinging to the last remnant before she spent the rest of her life behind bars.

"Let's get inside as quickly as we can," Finn murmured.

"And then you're getting more healing magic," I said. "What I gave you only patched you up."

"I can heal myself with enough time." He kept a tight grip on Karina's arms as he propelled her in front of him and through the doors.

"There's no need to play the hero," I said.

"Says the cat with blood in her fur." Finn's gritted teeth and sweaty brow revealed just how much he suffered. "I'll take five minutes once I know Karina can't harm anyone else."

There was a fizzing noise, and a small fire erupted in the reception area.

"That's enough of that!" Finn swiftly stamped out the fire. "You're making things worse for yourself."

Karina hissed at him. "I have to get it out!"

"Talk to us. Did you lose control of your magic?" I asked her. "Is that why you killed Erick?"

She squirmed in Finn's arms until he lifted her off her feet.

"More binding magic, Juno!" he yelled. "I can't hold her for long."

I whirled out more power, covering Karina from head to toe. She was still ridiculously strong, despite our brutal battle. Her magic felt almost as old as mine. It writhed and pulsed against my power, looking for a weak spot. If she found one, she'd exploit it.

We swiftly guided Karina into the main office, and after a few seconds of stunned surprise, several angels came to help Finn and relieve him of his burden. Once Karina had been taken to a cell and secured, Finn dropped into his seat and closed his eyes.

"It was a hard fight, but I knew we'd win," I said.

"Did you feel her hag power?" Finn shook out his hands as if trying to flick away the remnants of Karina's magic. "Gross. Distorted. She's a broken hag. I feel sick to my stomach. Even my demon retreated. He wanted nothing to do with her, and he's never backed down from a fight."

"Her breakdown must be because of Erick," I said. "Perhaps Karina learned he'd moved on with someone else. She wanted to get serious, but he said he was too busy with his career. If he found someone else, Karina would have felt rejected."

"Rejected enough to do this?" Finn said. "All of Karina's friends said she was fine. She was annoyed for a week or two, but she knew Erick was obsessed with his work. Something else must have happened to make her go after him so viciously and then continue with her rampage."

"When Karina settles, we'll ask her," I said. "And we'll get the confession we so desperately need."

Cythera approached with speed the second she saw us. "Who have you brought in? And why do they keep setting fire to things?"

Finn gave Cythera a quick rundown of our surprising encounter with Karina.

Cythera's forehead was furrowed as she absorbed the information. "What about Langdon and Jazzi? They have a motive. If Erick turned down their request for money, they could have decided to get rid of him. They'd have inherited his estate. We also have Tempest on our suspect list."

"Spend time with Karina and come to your own conclusion," I said with a tired huff. "She's dangerously unstable."

"And a descendant of an original hag," Finn said. "That's rare magic and hard to control."

"She's not in control," I replied.

There were several yelps from the cells, and two angels dashed out, their feathers ablaze.

"Let's question Karina while she's in a cell," Finn said. "And we should increase the wards, since her magic is getting through."

Cythera's sharp gaze ran over Finn's weary form. "Take ten minutes. I'll deal with our new arrival." She stomped off.

"Coffee, chocolate, and more healing for you," I said to Finn. "And no protesting. Boss's orders."

Finn chuffed out a laugh. "You won't hear me complaining. Thanks for helping out back there."

"I'll always help you in a fight."

He eased himself slowly out of the chair and shuffled toward the kitchen. Once Finn had recharged with caffeine and sugar, and I'd tossed a few more healing spells at him, we joined Cythera in the cells. There was a heavy guard presence by the door, and several more angels lurked close by in case they were needed.

There were black scorch marks on the wall where Karina must have flung her magic in an effort to escape.

"She's not talking," Cythera said as we arrived.

"Let me try," I said. "I have ways to make anyone talk."

"No obliteration threats!"

"I only obliterate as a last resort," I said.

Cythera waved a hand at me. "I'm watching. And listening."

"Why were you setting fire to those houses?" I asked Karina. "Has someone done you wrong? You were after revenge?"

"No fires. Not me." Karina's voice was raspy and smoke damaged. Now her hag form had faded, she looked average. Short. Compact body. Dark hair.

Cythera startled. "Those are the first words she's uttered since I arrived."

"You need to brush up on your interrogation techniques," I said.

Finn shot me a warning look before focusing on Karina. "Has something gone wrong with your magic? Are you struggling to control it? Help is available if you're willing to accept it."

"I'm innocent! I've done nothing wrong." Karina started to pant. Her legs wobbled, suggesting she was about to collapse.

"Tell us about your relationship with Erick Farten," I said.

"Erick?" Her eyes flashed black for a second before returning to normal. "I haven't seen Erick in ages. Why do you want to talk about him?"

"Were you in a relationship?" Finn asked.

Karina nodded, and her shaking lessened. "We dated. He was too busy with his work to give me his full attention, though."

"Were you angry when the relationship ended?" I asked.

Karina focused on my question, magic shimmering around her. "I... I was. But I didn't love the guy. He was kind of a creep and had a gross, drippy nose. But he had money and sometimes made me laugh, so we went out. It was no big deal. I was mostly annoyed that he ditched me. Erick was hardly the catch of the year. Not even catch of the day."

"When was the last time you saw him?" Finn asked.

"I don't remember. Why the questions about Erick? I thought you brought me here because I've been setting fire to things. Which I haven't."

"Examine this wall," Cythera said. "You did this before we strengthened the wards enough to keep you inside the cell."

Karina blinked several times and looked at her hands, turning her palms to the floor and back again. "I'd never do that. I use fire magic, but I've never been in trouble with the law. How did I get here? The last few minutes are hazy."

"I'd say it's more than a few minutes of memory haze causing you confusion," I said. "After you attempted to obliterate me and my angel companion, we flew you here."

"Flew? Obliterate?" Karina shook her head. "You're mistaking me for someone else."

"You don't remember attacking us?" I asked.

"I... I remember being at home. I've not been well, so I've been taking it easy."

"What symptoms have you had?"

"Headaches and tiredness. And I keep going to sleep and waking up in different places. I think I'm sleepwalking, but I've never done that before."

"Where do you find yourself when you wake up?" I asked.

"Places I don't know," Karina said. "I'm always outside. I get back home as quickly as I can. I was thinking, if it didn't clear up in a few days, I'd get checked out."

"Have you ever visited Crimson Cove?" I asked.

"Is that where we are now?" Karina glanced around the cell.

"You've been seen in our town," Finn said. "You were here at the same time as Erick."

"So?"

"You're in a precarious position, Miss Bellow," Cythera said. "Honesty will make us more willing to help you."

"Honesty about what? What are you talking about?"

"Your hag magic," I said. "You lost control. You've been hurting people, including Erick."

"And we're back to Erick!" Karina said. "Why would I hurt him? What's happened to him?"

"Erick was murdered," I said.

Karina's mouth dropped open. She looked at her hands again, and a shudder ran through her. "That's why I'm in this cell? Do you think I killed him?"

"You were seen in town on the night he died," Finn said. "You've been struggling with your magic. You've also recently separated from Erick, and he ended the relationship. That gives you a reason for revenge. Did you come to town to speak to him in an attempt to reconcile?"

"No! I don't follow Erick around like some broken-hearted teenager. We broke up. I took a few days to get over it, and then I moved on. I had no plans to marry the guy," Karina said. "I can't believe he's dead, though. Who had a problem with him?"

"You did," Cythera said. "He broke your heart."

"I was never in love with Erick! I liked his money more than him. Besides, I'm not the marrying type. Sometimes, when I go full hag, it's intimidating, and I've never met a guy who can handle that. I was considering becoming a book spinster. Or a cat spinster. Maybe a baking spinster. But not a weirdo killer of ex-boyfriends who I didn't much like, anyway. That would be a waste of effort and no fun. Messy, too."

"You were an impressively scary sight when we dealt with you," I said.

Karina's eyebrows flashed up. "We fought while I was a hag, and you survived?"

I nodded at Finn. "We're an impressive duo."

She blew out a breath. "Sorry if I got rough. When the hag power gets me by the throat, I'm a nightmare. I can usually tell when she wants to bust out, so I lock myself down and let the wizened old terror have her hissy fit until she calms."

"Not this time," I said.

"Your friends and work colleagues haven't seen you for several days. Where have you been?" Finn asked.

Karina looked perplexed. "I needed to get away and recharge, so I rented a tiny cabin in the woods. I've been busy at work and had a ton of social events. I was burning out. When I'm tired, my magic misbehaves. But never like this. And I don't turn to murder."

"I'll need the details of this cabin," Cythera said.

Karina gave her the information, and Cythera passed the address to two angels to investigate immediately.

"May I examine your magic?" I asked.

"How would you do that?" Karina's expression grew cautious.

"I'll need to touch you. I can feel magical bonds, so I can tell if there's a distortion in your energy."

"That's too risky," Cythera said. "There are layers upon layers of magical wards around the cell to ensure Karina's magic can't harm my angels."

"Then I'll go inside. No one else needs to be put at risk."

"Are you sure you want to do that, Juno?" Finn asked. "It took both of us to bring Karina down."

"I won't do anything bad," Karina said. "I'm sorry if I hurt you, but I don't remember doing it. Maybe... maybe there is something wrong with my magic. If there is, I want it fixed. I don't want to hurt anyone else."

"Get out of the cell at the first sign of trouble," Finn said to me. "If you're injured, Zandra will never forgive me."

"You have my word." I waited until Cythera made a small hole in the magic wards for me to slip through. The second I entered the cell, I wanted to run. The air was thick with the stink of broken magic. It curdled in my stomach and made me want to gag. I lightly pressed a paw against Karina's calf and almost blacked out.

"It's bad, isn't it?" Karina whispered.

"Your magic feels as if it's been torn apart and put back together wrong," I murmured. "You need immediate healing."

"How did it happen? Who did this to me?"

"Have you used any new potions or charms? Anything that could have caused such a devastating kink in your energy?" I asked.

Karina shook her head. "I've just been doing what I always do. What's wrong with me?"

"We'll find out. I'll use healing magic to hold things together, but angel healing will speed things up. Cythera, we must help Karina before it's too late to save her."

Cythera nodded. "If you make one wrong move, you'll get no more help from us. And I'll make it my personal mission to see you never leave a prison cell while you still have breath in your body."

I blinked in surprise. That was quite some threat. Cythera must be worried.

"I understand. I'll barely breathe while you heal me," Karina said.

"It's not a cure, just a short-term reprieve," I said.

Cythera lowered the magical wards even more so she could enter, approaching Karina with caution. Karina held her breath. She didn't even blink as we washed wave upon wave of healing angel and demigoddess magic over her. Angel healing was an extraordinary thing and more powerful than I could offer, so I was grateful Cythera had seen sense.

Karina swayed as she was wrapped in the magic, and although she occasionally twitched and growled, the unstable hag power faded to a more tolerable level, and I stopped feeling queasy.

By the time we'd finished getting Karina stable, I'd sunk onto my belly, and Cythera was leaning against the wall, a sheen of sweat on her forehead.

Karina gulped and cautiously shook out her hands. "Could you feel what was wrong with me?"

"Whatever it was, it's deeply infected you," I said. "And it's still in there."

"Is that why I've been losing time? Waking up in strange places? Feeling so off?"

"That wasn't hag magic we had to quell," Cythera said.

I nodded my agreement. Karina had been polluted with something distorted and rank with corruption.

"Was this magic the reason I went after Erick?" Karina whispered. "Did I really kill him? I don't remember. I can't be guilty if I don't remember, can I?"

I felt sorry for her. If she'd fallen under a dangerous spell, she may not have been in control of her hag abilities. Where would that leave her in the eyes of Angel Force?

"You should rest for now," I said.

"How can I rest? I must have done terrible things." Tears trickled down Karina's cheeks. "And I remember starting the fires. They were my fault. How will my neighbors forgive me?"

"Take it easy," Cythera said. "We have a few things to work through. We'll be back soon."

Once the magic wards were in place, we left Karina in her cell and headed to the main office.

"Finn, let Jazzi and Langdon go. We have our prime suspect," Cythera said.

He nodded and headed off to process the paperwork.

The angels Cythera had sent to visit Karina's rented cabin returned in a rush of warm air and cinnamon scent, a gleam of excitement shimmering on their faces.

"Did you find anything useful?" Cythera asked.

"We did! You'll want to take a look," one of them said. "There's evidence to prove Karina was obsessed with Erick. She must be our killer!"

Chapter 21

Cabin fever

I stood in a wooden cabin, staring at what could only be described as a stalker board. There were dozens of photographs of Erick pinned to the board.

"Karina has been busy." Finn stood beside me, Cythera next to him.

After we'd received word that the angels had found evidence pointing to Karina's guilt, we'd magicked ourselves to the cabin.

"So much for Karina taking time out to recharge," I said. "She came here to obsess over Erick and plan her final, devastating move."

"Karina played us. She made us think she was under the influence of something dark when it was her all along." Cythera scowled at the photographs, her arms crossed over her chest.

"There is gross magic attached to her. And it's not hag magic." I sniffed the air and twitched my booping snooter. There was an odd smoky smell, and it wasn't coming from the incense burners dotted around the property, although the heady remnants of the incense almost masked the smoke.

"Whatever the magic is, she's to blame," Cythera said. "She must have gained access to a different kind of power and used it to ruin Erick."

My gaze flickered around the room. "Why would someone with such substantial magic need more?"

"We'll find out when she's interviewed more thoroughly."

"This evidence should be enough to charge Karina," Finn said. "We have witnesses who saw her in Crimson Cove around the time of Erick's murder and now this creepy board. Karina must have been watching Erick ever since they broke up."

"Waiting to make her move," Cythera said.

I was quiet as I paced the cabin.

"You don't think it was Karina?" Finn followed me.

"I think I'm missing something, but I'm unsure what." I paused by the front door as a flash of something small and dark shot into the woods. I nudged open the door with my head and stepped outside. Everything was silent. No wind rustling the leaves or birds tweeting. What manner of creature had passed through the woods that made everything fall silent?

My hackles rose. Something was watching this cabin. I couldn't see what it was, but my instincts were never wrong. Whatever it was, it wasn't friendly, and I wanted it nowhere near me.

"Finn, arrange for this evidence to be collected," Cythera said from the bedroom. "I'll go back to

Angel Force and question Karina. As far as I'm concerned, this case is closed."

I kept scanning the woods, an unsettled feeling churning in my stomach. "It would appear so."

❧❧❧❧❧ ❧❧❧❧❧

I sat at a large table in the pizza parlor the next evening. Zandra was there, of course, along with Tempest and Wiggles. The three foster kittens were with us, too. Sage and Vorana had also joined us. Sage was settled on Vorana's lap, shooting threatening glares at the kittens whenever they moved.

Just after we'd ordered, Finn and Brodie strode through the entrance. Vorana gave Brodie a tired greeting and hugged him.

"Is everything good?" Brodie asked Vorana. "You look pale."

"Just busy," Vorana said. "And I was too tired to cook, which is why we're here."

"Finn said you were eating out tonight." Brodie looked concerned as he studied Vorana's face. "Is it work?"

"The bookstore is fine. Everything's fine," Vorana said. "We've already ordered, so we won't have long to wait for food. Don't worry about me."

"It's my job to worry, babe. I want to make sure you're okay."

It was touchingly sweet to see such a fierce, intimidating warrior angel be so gentle with his partner. Brodie often worked away, but Vorana and

Brodie had gotten closer recently. Perhaps there'd soon be another wedding to enjoy.

I turned my attention to Finn. "Has Karina confessed?"

"We're charging her, even though she keeps saying she's innocent," Finn said. "The stalker board clinched it for us. Karina seemed so surprised we'd discovered it and said she had no idea it was in the cabin."

"But she admits to making it?"

Finn shook his head. "She's sticking to her story that she wasn't that into Erick."

"If you hadn't filled me in on the case, I'd have believed her," Brodie said. "I sat in on the last interview. Karina should be on the stage. Her innocent act is incredible."

"I'm just glad Angel Force made the sensible choice and didn't charge me with Erick's murder," Tempest said.

"It was a close call," Finn replied, his smile fading. "We still don't know why Erick wrote that word in the dirt before he died."

"So long as you know it wasn't my name," Tempest said.

"We got our woman," Finn said. "A confession would make this a neat ending, but we have what we need."

One of the kittens sneezed, setting fire to a stack of paper napkins.

Wiggles growled at the kitten. "We should have left them at home. They cause so much chaos."

"You're jealous because they're outshining you," Tempest said.

I was surprised by her sharp tone. Wiggles could be exasperating, but Tempest always had his back, no matter what mischief he got into.

Wiggles grabbed several large chunks of garlic bread appetiser off a plate, hopped off his seat, and stalked out the door, his tail down.

I headed out after him. "Don't let the kittens get to you."

Wiggles spat out the garlic bread and sniffed it. "I don't get why everyone thinks they're sweet. They're troublemakers. I don't like them."

"You were a troublemaker when you were a pup. You sometimes still are."

Wiggles grunted as he pushed a piece of garlic bread my way.

I settled next to him as he ate. "Things have been weird lately, haven't they?"

He looked up, his mouth full, and mumbled something I didn't catch.

"Tempest still seems tense. And the household has been disrupted by those kittens. I think they're the reason Vorana's been so tired. She keeps running around after them."

Wiggles swallowed a large mouthful. "They're not coming with us when we go back to Willow Tree Falls. I've already told you that."

I sat in silence for a moment, watching the world go by, just as it always did. "How's Tempest?"

"Fine."

"Really?"

Wiggles belched a waft of garlic in my face. "Maybe she's not quite right, but she will be when we're home. Everything will be fine. Life just got messy. It happens."

"I'm sure it will be fine, especially now the demon prison is back under your control." I was relieved Zandra had returned unscathed from tackling the prison breakout with the other Crypt witches. She'd stunk of sulfur and had clearly used an enormous amount of magic, since she'd slept the whole night through without stirring, but my wonderful witch had triumphed, as I knew she would.

"That's the problem behind Tempest's weird behavior and her vanishing act," Wiggles said. "She's sensitive around demons. It's nothing else."

I waited for him to eat another chunk of bread, so I'd have time to get my point across. "Are you sure? Tempest has been around demons most of her life and has never acted like this before. And when you first showed up, you were frantic with worry."

Someone clearing their throat made me look over. Randal stood close by, shuffling his feet, his hands stuffed in his pockets.

"Give me a moment," I said to Wiggles and headed over to Randal. "You've heard the news about Karina?"

He nodded. "I was surprised. I know Karina. I always thought she was sweet, even with the whole hag thing. And her breakup with Erick wasn't bad. What do you think happened to her?"

"Her magic went rogue," I said. "That's what the angels believe. It felt toxic when I helped her."

"I guess it must have done. Strange though. Karina had a handle on her hag. She had a routine that kept things stable. Still, what do I know?" Randal shrugged. His gaze went to the pizza parlor. "How's Zandra?"

"I suspect she still needs time before she's ready to speak to you. She can be stubborn, and she's got a lot going on."

Randal chewed on his bottom lip. "It might be time I moved on. Maybe even have a change of scene. A guy can only pine after a woman for so long before it gets embarrassing, and I passed the embarrassing stage a long time ago."

"I'd be sorry if you left," I said. "Zandra would be, too."

"I like this town, but maybe it's for the best." He looked back at Zandra. "You never really know a person, do you?"

"You know Zandra well enough."

"I meant Karina. She seemed normal. I knew she had hag powers, but she was always so sensible and careful. She'd been trained in how to control them, so to go off the rails like that seems weird. Not natural."

"Something dark attached itself to Karina. She must have made a mistake and let in a twisted power. Angel Force is looking into what it could be, but they're not optimistic they'll find out. Some powers are deliberately tricky," I said. "The evidence in the cabin Karina rented revealed everything."

"The cabin?"

"Yes, that was where we found the board covered in Erick's pictures," I said.

"You mean the company cabin?"

I looked up at Randal. "That cabin belongs to Dilbert Innovations? The company Erick worked for?"

Randal scratched his chin. "I think so. At least, Erick said there was a place in the woods he'd go when he needed to work without interruption. Maybe the company owns it. It's remote. Cut off from anywhere. I remember him saying he took a girl there once or twice, although it doesn't sound all that romantic."

My heart pitter-pattered. "What time is it?"

"It's almost six. Why?"

"There's someone I must speak to. Wiggles, you're with me."

"What about the pizza?"

"You've devoured your own weight in garlic bread. We must hurry."

Randal stepped back. "Wait! Where are you going?"

"If Zandra asks where I am, tell her I'll be back soon." I placed a paw on Wiggles' head and translocated us to Dilbert Innovations.

Wiggles burped and shook out his fur. "I never translocate after I've eaten. It rarely ends well. What are we doing here? And where is here?"

As I'd hoped, the office was emptying out for the evening, dozens of workers eager to get home to a decent meal and a night lounging on the couch.

"There she is!" I said.

Sylvia hurried out, her purse slung over one arm as she walked away, head up.

"Who is she? And is she taking us to dinner?" Wiggles asked. "I'm not missing the pizza party."

"Sylvia was sweet on Erick. He wasn't interested in her, but Karina revealed she'd backed away from pursuing Erick because there was another woman on the scene."

"This is the other woman?"

"We need to ask her. Perhaps Sylvia wasn't so accepting of Erick's lack of interest," I said.

"And when we spoke to her, she was quick to deflect attention onto her boss, Dilbert."

Wiggles kept looking over his shoulder. "I've got the neck itches."

I sidled away from him. "Do you need a flea treatment?"

"No! Those little critters don't like the way I taste. I always get that itching neck feeling whenever I'm being watched," Wiggles said. "Recently, it's been happening more and more."

I glanced at him. "A demon?"

"No, they're never that subtle. If they want something from you, they try to rake it out with their claws," he said. "This has been happening when I'm on my own. It's as if I'm being stalked."

"An old enemy?"

"I don't know, but I don't like it." Wiggles growled, and his eyes glowed red.

I looked behind us. There was no one obviously following. If Wiggles had a stalker, they must be discreet. "We'll deal with your troublesome shadow later."

Wiggles huffed out smoke. "I hope this won't take long. The pizzas will be ready by now. That garlic bread didn't touch the sides."

"Our quickness depends on how cooperative Sylvia is," I said.

By now, we'd left the work district and were walking in a residential area. Sylvia headed to a compact apartment complex and went inside. We swiftly followed, getting through the door just before it shut, and ran up a short flight of stairs.

"Sylvia! Greetings. I'm glad I caught you," I said.

She jumped and dropped her keys. "Oh! Hello. How do you know where I live?"

"It's no secret, is it?" I asked. "I wanted to ask you about the cabin."

Sylvia's tongue darted across her bottom lip. "What cabin?"

"The one Erick used when he needed a quiet space to work on his designs," I said. "You manage the bookings, don't you? You said you do everything for Mr. Dimitri, including handling the company's accommodation needs."

"I... I don't know what you mean. I must get inside." She fumbled with her keys, almost dropping them again.

"Dilbert Innovations owns a cabin in the woods."

"No, we don't have a cabin. I'm sorry, I don't know what to tell you. Good evening."

"Wait! If they don't own it, do you? You let Erick use it, so it made it easier to watch him," I said.

Sylvia's expression tightened. "I don't know what you're talking about. And we have a no pets policy in this block. I'll get in trouble if you don't leave."

We didn't move.

"It makes more sense if you owned the cabin," I said. "And you rented it to Erick's former girlfriend,

Karina, so she could relax and unwind when her hag power threatened to take over. Did she know about the cabin from Erick, or did you approach her and offer it, so it made it easier for you to frame her for murder?"

"I know nothing about a cabin. If you'll excuse me."

"There'll be property records," I said. "If Angel Force runs a search, they'll find the ownership is in your name, won't they? And the stalker board we found didn't belong to Karina, but was your creation, wasn't it?"

"Do you want me to bite her?" Wiggles muttered. "She looks jumpy. And I think she's about to run."

Sylvia yanked a lump of quartz out of her purse. She blew on it and tossed it in the air. There was a loud bang and a huge flash of blinding light. By the time the flash had cleared, Sylvia had bolted and was sprinting down the hallway.

Wiggles shook himself, smoke puffing from his nostrils. "She thinks she can outrun us?"

"She's not just running." I caught a shimmer of magic around Sylvia as she raced for the emergency stairwell. "She's warding herself."

Wiggles snarled and launched forward, paws skidding on the smooth floor before he gained traction.

I followed, magic sparking from my claws. We burst down the stairs, each leap taking me closer as Sylvia's footsteps echoed below. She spun, hurling a bolt of crackling red energy toward us.

I darted to the side as the blast missed me by a whisker. It hit the wall behind us, exploding with a force that sent shards of concrete flying. Wiggles yelped but stayed on course. He barreled after Sylvia, opening his mouth, and releasing a torrent of fire that roared down the stairs.

Sylvia twisted, pulling up a shimmering blue shield just in time. The flames splashed over it, heat radiating back at us.

Wiggles growled, showing his teeth.

Sylvia clenched her jaw, and her fingers glowed. She slashed the air, releasing tendrils of shadow that lashed out at us. I ducked, letting one crackle overhead, and pounced forward, my magic flaring. With a swipe of my murder mittens, I sent a wave of magic toward her, aiming for her legs. She squeaked as it connected, throwing her off balance long enough for Wiggles to dart in.

He snapped his jaws around Sylvia's ankle, his fire searing through her wards and making her scream. She kicked, sending him rolling away. With a roar, Sylvia thrust both hands forward, another lump of quartz channeling her power, sending a massive wave of force hurtling toward us.

I sprang up the side of the wall, claws digging in as I narrowly avoided the blast. Wiggles took the hit, though, skidding back but regaining his footing, eyes blazing.

I angled toward Sylvia's blind spot. I unleashed a beam of white-hot magic at her back. She spun, barely shielding herself, but I'd already pounced, murder mittens digging into the shield, cracking it with my magic.

"Give up!" I hissed. "You're making it worse for yourself. We know you killed Erick and framed Karina."

Sylvia breathed heavily, her shield flickering under the strain. "No! I didn't do it!"

"Then why run?"

"I have to. It's not safe!" Hot, foul smoke billowed around Sylvia.

"What's not safe?"

"They're here! I don't know what they want." With a desperate scream, she threw her power outward, forcing me to release my grip. But her power waned, and instead of running, Sylvia slumped down.

Wiggles and I circled, cornering her at the bottom of the stairwell.

She heaved out a pained sigh. "I... I don't know what's wrong with me."

"Did you murder Erick?" I asked.

"No! I... I don't know." With one last desperate flick of her wrist, Sylvia cast another spell, but I was faster, snapping a containment ward around her. She froze, bound in place as the magic tightened. Her eyes filled with fury, but she couldn't move, the last of her magic snuffed out by the ward.

Wiggles trotted over and nudged me, his fur singed in places, though he wore a triumphant grin. "I can definitely handle pizza now."

"In a minute." A familiar scent hit me. It was a faint, smoky tang that lingered in the air, curling around us like invisible fingers. I stiffened, my booping snooter flaring as I tried to place it. It was the same smell I'd caught at the cabin. It wasn't incense. It was something darker, something unnatural.

I glanced at Sylvia. Her gaze was a mixture of confusion and defeat. She blinked, as if trying to clear her vision, and for the first time, I noticed a flicker of bewilderment behind her eyes. "Is there something you need to tell us?"

Sylvia's brow furrowed. "I didn't do it. At least, I... I don't remember. I've been forgetting a lot lately."

Wiggles huffed out his disbelief. "That's the oldest trick in the book, faking memory loss. Your purse is full of quartz. You planned to go into battle with these charged stones. You knew we'd be coming for you."

She shook her head. "I never use quartz to channel my power. I just found it in there."

My fur prickled, and something deep in my gut told me this wasn't a trick. I took a cautious step forward, sniffing the air. The smoky scent was still there, clinging to Sylvia's skin like an invisible shroud.

"What were you doing the night of Erick's murder?" I asked quietly, watching her closely.

She blinked again, her mouth opening as if to respond, but then her gaze went distant, unfocused, as if she were fighting against a memory buried too deep. "I... I was... I don't know. Everything's foggy."

I shot Wiggles a glance, and his expression softened, his tail lowering. This magic user was deeply troubled.

"Sylvia, did anyone give you anything unusual? A charm, a spell? Anything strange?" I asked.

Her gaze was almost desperate as she searched her memory. "I don't think so."

If she'd been under the influence of something dark, if someone had twisted her intentions, then the entire setup—the cabin, the stalker board, even her behavior—might have been orchestrated by someone else. But who?

At first, I'd thought it was Dilbert. Then Erick's siblings. Karina had been next in the frame, but I'd been niggled with uncertainty about her guilt. The cabin clue led us to Sylvia, but she was as confused as Karina. Were they both excellent actors? And how was the smoky stench I kept encountering connected?

Wiggles let out a low growl. "I'm confused. Is she guilty or not?"

I took one last look at Sylvia. "That's for the angels to decide."

Sylvia sagged, tears glistening in her eyes. "If I hurt Erick, I didn't mean to."

Wiggles stretched, yawning like he was trying to shake off the tension. "That sounds like a case closed to me. Can we go for pizza before I eat my own tail?"

I looked out at the darkened street, the smoky scent still twisting in the air like a warning. "Pizza and puzzles. The perfect pairing."

Chapter 22

New day

"I'd say it's been fun, but that would be a giant lie." Tempest stood outside Vorana's house with Wiggles beside her as they prepared to head home.

"At least you can't say you were bored." Zandra hugged her.

"I've had worse imprisonments. And Vorana knows how to cook. That's when she's not burning stuff." Tempest stepped back.

"We'll get her electrics fixed in time for your next visit," I said.

Tempest shrugged. "I'm not sure when that will be. This town is almost as troubled as Willow Tree Falls."

"All Crypt witches know how to handle trouble. It's what you're made for," I said.

"You're still here." Cythera swooped down and landed in front of us.

"And I can tell how happy you are about that." Tempest raised a hand. "Relax. I stayed overnight after you finally got the right person for Erick's murder, all thanks to my sister and Juno. We're leaving today. Right now, in fact. Got me a leaving gift, did you?"

Cythera scowled at Tempest. "I haven't forgotten you lied to me."

"About what?"

"You said you didn't know Erick, yet you met him at a conference."

"We've been over this. I mainly slept through that conference. Forget about it."

"Erick wrote the word Tempest in the dirt before he died."

"That's a loose end you'll have to tie up. This family is done fixing your incompetence."

Zandra sucked in a breath at the sharpness in Tempest's voice.

"You can understand why it raised questions from Angel Force," I said. "You also concealed your demon-hunting assignment on the night of the murder." That was a puzzle I'd yet to get to the bottom of, and it could still cause Tempest trouble if she couldn't pull the right strings when she got home.

Wiggles growled. "You know it wasn't Tempest. Move on. We got the weird stalker chick. She almost got away, but we were too smart for her."

I should leave Tempest alone, but much like Cythera, this situation still felt unsettling, and I needed to find out why. If Tempest wasn't stable, I couldn't have her around Zandra. They were sisters, but I'd protect Zandra from any source of danger.

Randal appeared at the end of the street and headed toward us. He slowed when he saw we were talking to Cythera, turned around and hurried away.

Tempest also noticed and laughed. "Why don't your angels go hassle Zandra's guy? He was the one who brought this trouble to town. Maybe he's not such a nice guy after all."

"Randal is innocent!" I protested. "He was knocked out, and his friend is still in the hospital."

"A falling out between friends can be as sharp as any weapon," Tempest said. "Besides, if he hadn't invited Erick here, none of this would have happened. These angels want someone to pick on, but they need to find themselves another target, because I'm not playing."

"Steady," Zandra cautioned.

"Why should I go easy on them? I'm done with being treated like the bad witch," Tempest said. "Are you surprised I stayed away this long, when this is the welcome I get?"

"I've treated you fairly," Cythera said after an awkward pause. "I go by reputation."

"Yeah, whatever. And mine stinks. Let's get out of here, Wiggles." She nudged Zandra with her elbow. "See you around."

Zandra nodded, and I waved a paw at Wiggles as they vanished in a flash of translocation magic.

"How's Karina?" I asked Cythera, who still stared at the spot Tempest had been standing in.

"Troubled. She's at the hospital under guard while the doctors figure things out."

"And Sylvia? She needs treatment, too."

"I know! Specialist healers are arriving this afternoon. They'll look at Karina and Sylvia to see if

265

they can puzzle through what conflicted with their magic."

"Sylvia will be charged with Erick's murder?" I asked.

"That's the plan."

"Even though she won't confess?" Zandra said.

"We don't need a confession. The evidence tells us the truth."

"What about the source of the magic?" I asked.

Cythera flicked a wing in my direction. "Sylvia got in over her head. She was obsessed with Erick and couldn't have him. She must have tried a love spell that went wrong. It turned her to compulsive thoughts about Erick, and those thoughts drew her to try darker spells. One corruption led to another. It's a slippery path."

"Did you find the love spell Sylvia used? Where did it come from?" I asked.

"Stop asking questions! I have what I need. Erick's killer is about to be charged. You should congratulate me, not look for problems that aren't there."

I wasn't being put off by Cythera's increasingly surly tone and wing fluttering. "Did Sylvia tell you the spell she used on Erick, Charlie, and Randal? If you can find that information, you should be able to help Charlie."

Cythera grunted. "These things take time."

"You're not short on angels. Or we could lend a paw."

"We need to get back to work," Zandra said. "Barney's been generous, but we're pushing our luck by missing another day."

I sighed. Zandra had a point, but I didn't like all the threads of unfinished business flapping in the breeze. It made me uneasy. A neat, tidy solution was the way to go, but this resolution left a sour taste on my tongue.

There was a yelp from inside Vorana's house, and she dashed outside, Sage behind her. "The kettle blew up! Hot water blasted everywhere."

The kittens bounded out a second later and chased each other around the front yard, weaving between bushes and batting at fallen leaves. One kitten fixed on Cythera and jumped at her face, missing completely and bouncing off her chest.

Cythera barely spared the kitten a glance. "Now trouble has left town, I have work to do."

"On fixing your attitude," Zandra muttered.

Cythera glared at her then took to the wing and shot out of sight.

Vorana held a damp cloth in one hand as she joined us. "More trouble with Angel Force?"

"Just Cythera being Cythera," Zandra said. "She needs to get over herself. And the word thanks has left her vocabulary again."

"Let's go to Sorcha's café to celebrate the case finally being solved," Vorana said. "I don't trust any of the appliances in my house. Until the repair guy has been here and checked over everything, I'm only serving cold food and drink."

"Sorcha's it is," I said.

Sage yowled as she was set upon by the kittens. I dashed over and heaved them off.

"Careful! They're using their claws." Sage slashed and growled until the kittens gave up the fight and bowled away to find someone else to pester.

Watching them, I struggled to smile. The case had been solved, but I still felt like I was missing something.

"What's up with you?" Sage inspected her side.

"Nothing. Well, this mystery. It doesn't feel like it's over. Charlie is still in the hospital."

"Can't the doctors fix him?"

"Cythera is bringing in healers for everyone caught up in this case."

"Then he'll soon be on the mend." Sage finished her inspection and seemed happy the kittens hadn't done too much damage. "You should be excited about going to Sorcha's for breakfast. I love Vorana, but lately, the food has been iffy."

"I am. Sorcha's smoked salmon is excellent."

"When we're there, the kittens can bother other people while I eat." Sage sidled along beside me as we followed Zandra and Vorana into town. "I can tell you're still not happy."

"There's no confession." I sighed. "It's not the perfect conclusion, but it might be the best we'll get."

"It does sound messy." Sage zapped a kitten who'd foolishly decided to stalk her.

"Perhaps."

"No perhaps. And there are too many messes in Crimson Cove. It's making me uneasy."

"Such as?"

"Vorana's exploding appliances."

"That is unfortunate."

"The kittens."

"A temporary mess. Someone will soon fall in love with them and take them off my paws."

"Reports of weird magic in town."

I paused. "That's true. Sorcha had me help her with a problem at the café. Someone had placed a spell on her appliances."

Sage hesitated. "Tempest."

I glanced at Sage. "Meaning?"

"You felt it, too. Her magic is out of whack. I avoided her as much as possible because her power gave me the chills. Wiggles even spoke to me about it."

"I'm monitoring that situation. It's most likely nothing."

"What about the secret you're still keeping from Zandra? Now Tempest and Wiggles are no longer under the shadow of this murder charge, Zandra will want to know about the enchanted bracelet you gave her," Sage said. "Unless you're planning on whisking us all off to another spa so you can hide from her, you'll have to confront this problem soon."

"I did enjoy our last spa vacation. I should look for last-minute deals."

Sage huffed out a breath. "As I said, too many messes. Messes cause problems."

"Barely any problems. And if we try hard enough, everything can be fixed."

"You mean patched over or ignored. That's not a solution." Sage zapped another kitten who was on its belly, butt wriggling, and eyes wide. "I know three things I'd like to fix permanently. If you're not dealing with the Zandra issue, help me get rid of these kittens once and for all."

"Sage. You can't mean—"

"No! I'm not a monster. But they need a home far from here, so I won't get jumped on, set fire to, or have my kibble stolen."

"If I make the rehoming a priority, will you get off my back about Zandra?"

She grunted. "For a while. But you can't avoid it forever."

"I don't need forever, just for now." I gently nudged my grumpy friend with my head. "So, what delicious food shall we order at Sorcha's café?"

About the author

K.E. O'Connor (Karen) is a cozy mystery author living in the beautiful British countryside. She loves all things mystery, animals, and cake.

When she's not writing, she volunteers at a local animal sanctuary, reads a ton of books, binge watches mystery series, and dreams of living somewhere warmer.

To stay in touch with the mysteries, where the killer always gets caught, justice is served magic style, and the familiars talk, join her newsletter.

Newsletter:
www.subscribepage.com/cozymysteries
Website: www.keoconnor.com
Facebook: www.facebook.com/keoconnorauthor

Also by

Witch Haven: Welcome to Witch Haven, where nothing is what it seems. Meet four fabulous witches as they struggle with their destinies, deal with misfiring magic, murder, and the Magic Council.

Crypt Witches: Meet Tempest Crypt, a witch who swallows demons, and Wiggles, her mini talking hellhound, while you enjoy magical murder and intrigue.

Lorna Shadow: A cozy mystery series set in the fun world of a personal assistant who sees ghosts. Meet Lorna, her ditzy sidekick, Helen, and Flipper, the dog who senses ghosts, as they solve crimes and save the day.

Holly Holmes: An adorable cozy culinary mystery series set in the beautiful village of Audley St. Mary. Each book is full of treats, murder, and twists. Join Holly and Meatball, her clue-hunting dog, as they solve murders and eat cake.